W9-BTZ-709

RABBIT
FOOT
BILL

ALSO BY HELEN HUMPHREYS

FICTION
Leaving Earth
Afterimage
The Lost Garden
Wild Dogs
Coventry
The Reinvention of Love
The Evening Chorus
Machine Without Horses

NON-FICTION
The Frozen Thames
Nocturne
The River
The Ghost Orchard

HELEN HUMPHREYS

RABBIT FOOT BILL

A NOVEL

HarperCollins
Publishers Ltd

Rabbit Foot Bill
Copyright © 2020 by Helen Humphreys.
All rights reserved.

Published by HarperCollins Publishers Ltd

First edition

No part of this book may be used or reproduced in any manner
whatsoever without the prior written permission of the publisher,
except in the case of brief quotations embodied in reviews.

HarperCollins books may be purchased for educational, business,
or sales promotional use through our Special Markets Department.

HarperCollins Publishers Ltd
Bay Adelaide Centre, East Tower
22 Adelaide Street West, 41st Floor
Toronto, Ontario, Canada
M5H 4E3

www.harpercollins.ca

Library and Archives Canada Cataloguing in Publication
Title: Rabbit Foot Bill : a novel / Helen Humphreys.
Names: Humphreys, Helen, 1961- author.
Identifiers: Canadiana (print) 2020018539X
Canadiana (ebook) 20200185403
ISBN 9781443451543 (hardcover) | ISBN 9781443451567 (ebook)
Classification: LCC PS8565.U558 R33 2020 | DDC C813/.54—dc23

Printed and bound in the United States of America
LSC/H 9 8 7 6 5 4 3 2

FOR HUGH LAFAVE AND CAROL DRAKE

BASED ON A TRUE STORY

CANWOOD

—

SASKATCHEWAN
1947

BILL NEVER LIKES TO LEAVE TOWN THE same way twice. He strides out with an urgency I find hard to match. He leads me through the tamarack woods. He leads me through the meadow bog. He leads me through the tall prairie grasses. He leads me across the swift, shallow river. I usually have to run to keep him in my sight.

We have been friends for a year, Bill and I, and although people don't approve, we are friends anyway. I like that Bill isn't bothered by what people say. Mostly he is just worried that someone will follow him out of town and see where he lives.

The reasons why people don't like my being friends with Bill are these: first, because he is a man and I am a twelve-year-old boy; and second, because he is a man who is not like other men. He doesn't talk much. He doesn't live in a house. He doesn't have a real job. He doesn't have a family. People say he's slow, but as I've already said, I have to run to keep up with him.

3

No one blames me for the friendship. They see it as Bill's doing. But really, it is me who pushed for it. I followed him around on the days when he sold his rabbit's feet in town, or did odd jobs for Mrs. Odegard. I hounded him with questions. I fetched him water when he was hot and thirsty. I wore him down with my attentions so that now he's used to having me around.

"Why do you want to befriend a tramp?" asks my father, and I can't tell him why. I can't explain this feeling of running after Bill under the long, blue prairie sky. It is like he is leading me out of darkness, out of a loneliness I don't even know I have.

Bill lives in Sugar Hill. Right inside the hill. It takes ages to get there, so I don't go very often, as Bill has to walk me in and then walk me back out again before nightfall.

When we get to Bill's house, I'm always out of breath from rushing. Near Sugar Hill I can hear his dogs barking, and when we are in sight, they come running up to greet us. There's a black dog and a grey, shaggy one. Bill doesn't have names for them. He puts his hand on their heads—first the black dog, then the grey one—and they stop barking and follow us into the house.

The house is carved into the base of the hill. There's a small wooden door that Bill can only get through by ducking down, but inside the house he can stand up straight again. The dug-out space is framed up with pieces of wood and there are walls made from the large wooden grain dividers from the rail cars.

There's a big main room with two pockets off it. One pocket is the kitchen and the other is the bedroom. The kitchen has pieces of corrugated tin around the walls, and a stove made from a forty-five-gallon oil drum with a fire hole cut out near the bottom and a metal sheet laid on the top so water can be boiled and food can be hotted up. A stovepipe leads from the barrel, through the earth overhead, and pokes up outside, like an animal nosing out of its burrow.

In the bedroom there is a bed made of hay bales and covered with rabbit skins. The main room has more hay bales for seats, and a bookshelf that covers one wall. Sometimes, if it's bright outside and Bill's left the door open for light, I will sprawl on the hay bales and look through his books.

What is wrong with not working? What is wrong with lying on the hay bales, on the soft rabbit fur, with the dogs curled up beside you, in the house you have made yourself? What is wrong with wanting to keep away from people? There's not much about people that I like either. I have only been in this town for two years, but that is long enough to have made friends and I haven't got any.

This will be the last time I come to Bill's house with him, but I don't know that yet. I have skipped school to be here.

It's early summer. Bill's garden at the base of the hill is coming into bloom. We have to walk through it to get to the house, and he shows me things as we follow the path up to the front door.

"Beets," he says, pointing to a patch of bare earth. "Rabbits ate the tops."

"Roses, carrots, onions." He stops in front of another square of empty dirt. "This is where the lettuce used to be," he says. "I blew it up trying to shoot the rabbits."

I circle Bill, like a fly on a horse. I want to be all around him, all at once.

"Bill," I say, "will you show me how to grow things? Will you take me hunting? Can I shoot a rabbit?"

Bill opens the door of the house, slouches down to fit inside the frame.

"Nope," he says, and steps inside.

He turns as I'm coming through the doorway and picks me up, his huge hands grabbing me around the ribs and hoisting me up into the air.

"Quieten down," he says, as though he's talking to the barking dogs.

The pressure of his hands around my ribs makes me squirm and kick out like a beetle. I can smell his sweat and the stale tang of his breath. He carries me over to the hay bales by the bookshelf and drops me.

We eat great slabs of bread with jam made from the Saskatoon berries that grow in the gullies between the hills. Bill brews tea in a saucepan and we drink it out of two battered tin mugs. After he's finished drinking his tea, Bill puts some freshly severed rabbits' feet to boil in the tea water. Boiling them gets rid of the stray bits of flesh and blood and the dirt from their nails from when they were alive. People only want to buy a clean rabbit's foot. It's not lucky if it's not clean.

"Can I have another one, Bill?" I ask. "I lost the one you gave me."

This isn't true. I have carefully kept all the rabbits' feet I've managed to make Bill give me. I have them lined up by size on the small table beside my bed. Sometimes, when I hold one in my hands, I push back the hair and feel each tiny toenail. It is the feel of the toenails that makes me remember that the foot was once alive.

"Last one," says Bill, and he walks over and drops a rabbit's foot into my cupped hands. "Next time I'll have to be charging you."

I know this isn't true either, but I pretend to take the warning.

"I can see that, Bill," I say, and I tuck the rabbit's foot into the pocket of my overalls.

After the murder I don't know what to do with the rabbits' feet. There are six of them altogether, enough for three full rabbits, since the only feet Bill uses for the charms are the hind ones.

What I wish, after the murder, when I'm lying alone

at night in my room, is not that the boy was alive again, but that the rabbits were. I lay the rabbits' feet out on my stomach. I can feel the cold, thin bones and the ticky-tack of their nails against my skin. I want them to be conjured back into three living rabbits, each one warm and trembling, resting quietly, safely, on my body.

Rabbits sleep in a great rabbit heap in their burrows. When Bill cuts the feet off his rabbits, he throws their bodies into a pile, ready for skinning. They seem asleep, furry body nestled into furry body, slung over one another in easeful abandon. They seem asleep until I look at their back legs and see the bloodied stick ends where their feet used to be attached.

"Why are rabbits' feet lucky?" I ask.

"Dunno." Bill has his back to me, trying to scoop the feet out of the boiling water before they disintegrate into soup.

"Is it because they're fast? Because they can outrun everything?" I'm thinking that a rabbit runs so swiftly that it could even outrun trouble. Perhaps that is why it's lucky to carry their dried-up, shrivelled feet in your pocket.

"They run fast, but they run to a pattern," says Bill. "And once you've sussed out the pattern, they're easy to catch." He turns around from the stove and holds out a small, sodden rabbit's foot towards me and smiles. "See."

Before it's time for me to return home, Bill walks me

up to the top of Sugar Hill. It is the highest point of land around, and looking down at the flat rectangles of fields and the squares of the grain bins makes me feel more bird than boy, like I could fly right off the top of Sugar Hill, soar lazily above the prairie dusk.

The dogs have come with us to the crest of the hill and they wrestle with each other in the vetch. I like watching them fight, because they mean it and don't mean it at the same time. They can stop right away if they decide to. When I am fighting it's not that simple.

The sun is lower than the hill, although it takes forever to sink beneath the flat pan of prairie in the long lean of light that takes afternoon to evening. At this moment we're the highest point in the landscape and I want to remark on this to Bill, but I can tell he's tired of my jabbering. He stands a little apart from me, arms at his sides.

It's June. The light is long, but the air shifts cool in the evenings. I can still taste the winter in it.

This was one of the last real times I spent with Bill, and I wish we had spoken or that he had laid his hand on my head as he sometimes did; but this didn't happen. I watched the dogs and he watched the sky, and then he turned and I followed him back down the hill.

He takes me to the edge of town and I walk along the rail lines until I'm home. We live at the station and this station looks the same as all the other stations we've lived in. One small prairie town is the same as the next to me, and I don't know why my father thinks they are different. He's restless, my mother said once. He has a restless soul. But how is moving twenty miles down a rail line a cure for this restlessness? The only thing that makes this place better than the last one is Bill. Sometimes, coming home at night to the station, I actually, seriously, forget which town I'm in.

Supper is cold beef and potato salad. Father doesn't like talk at meals, so we sit there in the cool of the kitchen with the night noise of the prairie outside and the rattle of knives and forks against our plates. My parents won't be finding out about my missing school until tomorrow, so tonight I am safe and I sink into the calm waters of this, into our quiet supper in the kitchen, followed by mother and I listening to the radio in the parlour and father sitting on the porch, smoking. I don't call it happiness, but looking back now I think it was a sort of happiness; that shelter is a kind of happiness.

At night there's the low loop of the train whistle and the scratch of bat wings in the air outside my bedroom window. I lie in the dark and listen to the sounds of this June night, and I wonder if Bill can hear these same things from deep inside Sugar Hill, or if he only hears the noises of the burrowing creatures that share the dugout with him. I wonder if the rabbits' souls are restless souls and if they try to claw their way out of the hole or race around at top speed inside, looking for their living bodies. Thinking of the rabbits makes me remember the rabbit's foot that Bill gave me this afternoon, and I get out of bed to fetch it from the pocket of my overalls. The floor is smooth and cold under my bare feet, and when I cross the room to the chair where my clothes are folded, I can see the moon, huge and heavy, weighing down the corner of my bedroom window. It keeps me there, hand curled around the bony rabbit's foot, my skin growing chill. It is not that I think the moon is beautiful—although I do like the milky sway of it—but more that I can feel the heaviness of it as though it is a sorrow suddenly caught in the snare of my own blood.

The next day at school I try to keep well away from the group of boys who are always beating on me for reasons I never understand. It's raining, so I must be hit. We're doing sums in arithmetic, so I must be hit. The sky is a certain shade of blue, so I must be hit.

I slink into the schoolyard just before the bell, keeping to the wall and lingering near a knot of girls playing hopscotch. When it's time to go into class, girls and boys are meant to line up separately before entering the building. I stay pressed to the brick wall until the last possible minute and then scuttle in at the end of the girls' line. Once inside the classroom it's safer because the teacher is there. Mrs. Clark likes order and carries a long wooden pointer, smacking it down on the edge of a student's desk if they start whispering or horsing around. She is not above using the pointer to hit a student's outstretched palms when they have been "disruptive." Mrs. Clark's words are connected very closely to certain punishments, and we have all quickly learned this vocabulary. Being "inconsiderate" means a half hour of standing quietly in the corner of the classroom, face to the wall. If a student is "unruly," they are sent to stand out in the hallway for an hour. But being "disruptive" means that the student is hauled up to the front of the class, told to put out their hands, and then whacked across the palms with the wooden pointer. Sometimes one hit is judged to be enough, but if Mrs. Clark has been particularly annoyed by the manner of the disruption, she will strike a student's hands until they are red and swollen.

Most of my fellow pupils are afraid of Mrs. Clark, but I am only grateful for her. While she is striding around the classroom or stiffly writing equations on the chalkboard, I am safe from harm. No one will pick on me while we are in class for fear of being seen to be "disruptive."

Today I am the last to file into the classroom, and as I come through the doorway, Mrs. Clark moves behind me to close the door.

"Where were you yesterday, Leonard?" she asks.

I have already rehearsed my lie on the walk to school and it slides easily out of my mouth.

"Helping my father at the station, ma'am," I say.

This is a farming community. Teachers are used to their pupils missing school for chores.

"Very well then," Mrs. Clark says. "But I will be needing a note from him next time."

"Yes, ma'am."

The door clicks shut behind me and I take my seat at my desk near the window.

I don't mind school. It doesn't take much effort to be good at it, and I can spend some of the day paying attention and some of it staring out the window at the fields. I like to think of Bill, imagine what he is doing while I am learning geometry or the provincial capitals. I like to picture him doing the most ordinary of things—walking with his dogs or eating breakfast. He does a handful of things over and over again, and I know what most of these things are. It makes me feel good to be able to recreate the activities of his daily life while I am sitting at my school desk.

Recess brings danger in the form of the older boys in class, who come sniffing for me like dogs after a rat. The pack of boys are led in their chase by a tall boy with the nickname of Snake, but whose real name is Sam Munroe.

I was last into the school and I am first out at recess, hurtling through the door and out into the yard, flattening myself against the brick wall by the hopscotch grids.

Sometimes the girls take pity on me and let me call out the numbers for them, but today I am outside before they have had a chance to assemble, and the group of bully boys is right behind me. I can hear their feet slapping against the ground as they race after me. It sounds just like wings on a flock of ducks beating up from a pond.

Snake grabs me around the neck, his hand sweaty and his breath oddly sweet. His angry face is just inches from mine as he pushes me up hard against the wall.

"Did you think you could escape your punishment?" he says.

It's not really a question, and I've learned, from past mistakes, not to answer him, even if he insists on it. Whatever I say will be wrong and will bring more trouble down on me. Instead, I pretend that I can't breathe, that he's cutting off my air supply. I gasp and splutter, hope that my face is turning suitably red. I flail my arms and legs.

And then, like a huge bird descending from the sky, like an angel from heaven, Mrs. Clark plucks Snake off me, and the other boys scatter like chicken feed. I rub my neck. It feels like a miracle, watching Snake be hauled along by Mrs. Clark, back through the door of the school for what is sure to be an energetic caning. But I also know that this moment of victory will be a short one, and that Snake will be after me twice as fiercely when he gets free from the teacher.

The hopscotch girls are out in the yard now. They circle me like crows. One of them, Sally, who has a desk near mine, puts her hand on my arm.

"Are you hurt?"

I shake my head. My neck feels a bit sore, but it's nothing compared to what I usually suffer under the hands of Snake and his friends. I feel lucky, not hurt.

Sally has kind brown eyes, and her frown is one of concern, not displeasure. I like the feeling of her hand on my arm.

"Why does he hate me?" I ask. "I haven't done anything to him."

"You're new," says Sally.

"Not that new," I say.

I have been in Canwood for two years. That seems like a suitably long time to me.

"You're new," she says again.

"And small," says one of the other girls.

And then I do understand. It's not about me at all. It's because I've recently arrived at the school, where probably there have never been any new students, any people outside of this small community, any strangers. And I am small for my age, making it easy to pick on me. Somehow, this makes me feel disappointed. I wish Snake's persecution was actually about me somehow, not just about aspects of my life I have no control over.

"It won't stop then, will it?" I say.

"Maybe you'll grow bigger," says Sally helpfully. She takes her hand off my arm. "Would you like to count for us until recess is over?"

The school is at the edge of town. If I walk through Canwood and out the other side, then along the dusty concession road, I will arrive back home, at the small farmhouse near the rail station, where we live now. If I head out in the opposite direction after leaving the school grounds, I can saunter through the open country-side all the way to Sugar Hill.

I decide to go home after school, rather than go in search of Bill. I have been lucky today, in not being caught out in my absence from yesterday and in having Mrs. Clark save me from Snake, but I can't count on that luck continuing. What is true one day often stops being true the next.

I'm a fast runner, so I can usually outrun any boy who wants to beat on me after school. But today I am safe, because Snake has been both whipped and kept behind in detention, and no one else has the inclination to give chase without his lead. I can saunter through the streets of Canwood, taking my time to get home, bend-ing down to pet a tabby cat, or looking in the windows of the hardware store, or lingering outside the gas sta-tion because I like the sound of the bell when cars drive over the rubber hose by the pumps.

Lucy Weber is out by her roses. When she sees me,

she waves me over. She's a friend of my mother's, comes to our house sometimes to sit with her on the porch after supper. I run across the road and up her driveway when she signals to me.

"Leonard," she says, "I think I've made a discovery."

She holds out her hand towards me. There's something small lying in her palm. I come across the lawn to get closer.

"That's a rosehip," I say. It seems odd that Lucy Weber wouldn't know about rosehips, since she grows roses.

She laughs. "Yes," she says. "But look at it closely. What does it resemble?"

I bend my head over the rosehip.

"It just looks like a rosehip," I say. Even if I squint and tilt my head, it doesn't look any different.

Lucy Weber sighs. "Where is your imagination, Leonard?" She points to the orange circle of the rosehip. "This looks like a body. And these." She touches the papery brown tendrils that attach to the orange circle. "These look like legs."

"An octopus," I say, suddenly seeing what she means.

"Yes. Why do you think that is?"

"An accident?" I can't think that a rosehip and an octopus have anything in common.

"There are no accidents in nature, Leonard," says Lucy Weber. "Just mysteries we don't know how to solve yet." She carefully places the rosehip in my hand. "Here. You can ponder on this mystery for yourself. Later. At your leisure."

I still think that it is more an accident than a mystery that the rosehip resembles an octopus, but I drop the rosehip into my pocket anyway. I like Lucy Weber and don't want to disappoint her by not being curious enough.

After Lucy Weber's, there are a few more streets of houses, then three enormous grain elevators, like giants, and then the town just ends. The houses on the last street empty onto the rail tracks, then grassland, and then there is just the scatter of farmhouses and the neat squares of the fields, continuing as far as I can see, out to the next village and beyond that one to the next, and so on, and so on. Forever. Amen.

The town we lived in before this one was called Shell Lake. It seemed bigger, or maybe that was just because I was smaller then. I remember that the water of the lake was circled by rushes and reeds, and that there was a forest out past the town. I went there once with my parents for an outing. I remember the way the trees talked to one another, all high up and whispery, full of secrets.

I am thinking this, thinking about the gossiping pine trees outside of Shell Lake, when I see a man crouched over in a cornfield. The ground is still turned from winter, the corn just planted, and so the field is bare and it is easy to spot the bent-over figure of Bill. I can't believe my luck! My feet fly over the stubble and lumps of earth to get to him.

"Bill!"

He looks up at my approach, grins at me. I run right into him and he circles my body with one of his strong arms, to both hug me and stop my forward momentum.

"What are you doing here?" I say.

Bill is not often on this side of the town. He usually keeps to the countryside around Sugar Hill. It is more wild and remote over there, fewer farms, less chance of meeting people.

"The rabbits will be after the corn," he says, holding up a loop of wire. "And I am after the rabbits."

"Can I help you set your snares?"

"Won't they be waiting for you at home?"

"Not yet." I can run all the way back after helping Bill and still make it home in time for supper.

"All right then." Bill sits back on his heels. "You ever set a snare before?"

"No."

"Well then, you'll have to be the rabbit."

Bill grabs an old cornstalk from beside him on the ground. He draws some lines in the dirt. They move in a zigzag pattern away from his boots.

"This is how a rabbit runs," he says. "So, if I'm about putting a snare here, where should the next one go?"

I look out over the field.

"Run it," says Bill. He gives me a little push. "Be the rabbit."

I race in a tight zigzag across the muddy field, over the rotting cornstalks and the nubs of stones, under the blue prairie sky. I run until my heart is banging against my ribs and my breath is tight in my throat, and then, when I run out of field, I race back to Bill.

He is threading one end of a length of wire through a small loop he has twisted in the other end of the wire, to make a large noose.

"Well," he says, not looking up from his task, "what did you learn about being a rabbit?"

"It's a bit dizzy-making."

"What else?"

"They can't see very far ahead because they are always turning instead of going in a straight line."

"Good. What does that tell us about a rabbit?"

Bill takes a thick piece of stick from the front pocket of his overalls and scrapes around in the dirt for a big enough rock to use as a hammer.

"I don't know."

"It tells us," says Bill, his hand closing round a fist-sized rock, "that they run to a panic, not a plan. It tells us"—he starts pounding the stick into the earth—"that they are used to being chased, that it is their natural state. Why is that?" He tests the immovability of the stick and then, satisfied that it is firmly embedded in the field, begins to twist one end of the wire noose around it.

"Because rabbits are prey animals?"

"Exactly." Bill balances the other end of the wire on a bit of cornstalk so that the noose is suspended over a furrow. He stands up and ruffles my hair with his hand. He has just been scrabbling around in the earth, so his hand is covered in dirt and bits of straw, but I don't care. I lean into him and he lets me.

"Go and be the rabbit again," Bill says. "Only this time, stop where you think the next snare should go, and I will come and meet you there."

I am home in time for supper, having run like a rabbit all the way from the cornfield to the farmhouse. My mother is in the kitchen. My father must still be at the station.

"Have you been fighting again?" My mother turns from the sink when I come into the room. "You're covered in dirt."

"Not fighting," I say. "Playing."

"Well, whatever you've been doing, go and wash up before supper."

The little window in the bathroom overlooks the back of the house and the fields beyond it. When I left Bill in the cornfield, he was still setting snares. I climb up on the edge of the bathtub so that I can look out of the window better. He's probably too far away to spot, but you can see a long way on the prairies, and so I look for any movement in the distant fields. I think I see the flutter of something dark on the horizon line, but it is so far away that it could just as easily be a crow as Bill.

"Leonard," calls my mother from the kitchen, "what are you doing in there? I don't hear any water."

When I come back into the kitchen, supper is on the table. There are only two plates of meatloaf and vegetables.

"We're not waiting for Daddy?"

"He has to work late. There are a lot of freights coming through tonight."

I like it when the trains rumble into the town at night. The tracks are close enough to the house that it shakes with the weight of the rail cars, making it feel as though I am on board the train, heading for somewhere exciting, away from the prairies and into a big city like Toronto or Montreal.

The meatloaf is recognizable as being formed from the leftover bits of cold beef from last night's supper. I poke at the block of it with my fork, separating out the squares of milky onion that I'm not keen on eating.

"Sorry," says my mother, watching my careful dissection of her labours. "I forgot. Would you like me to make you a cheese sandwich instead?"

Often I am forced to sit at the table until I have finished my meal, whatever it is. It doesn't matter if I don't like certain elements of it. But today feels like a magic day, and I am moving through it protected from anything I dislike or that causes me harm. Even my mother has fallen into line with this magic and doesn't seem bothered that she has to make me a second supper. She is humming by the stove as she grills my cheese sandwich.

After supper, I tell my mother I have homework so I can go and lie on my bed and think about setting snares with Bill in the cornfield, and wait for the trains to blow past the house, rattle the metal legs of my bed against the floor.

The next morning I run like a rabbit along the concession road, deke around the grain elevators by the rail tracks, then walk slowly through town towards school, whistling the song my mother was humming the night before.

When I turn the corner of Mrs. Odegard's street, I see Bill out front, clipping her caragana hedge. He sometimes does gardening work and odd jobs for the old people in town. The old people seem much more forgiving of his ways than the people his own age or the boys my age.

"Bill!"

I run the last few hundred feet to get to him as fast as I can. He doesn't stop his clipping, but looks over his shoulder at me and smiles. It's a hot morning already and it's not even nine o'clock yet. I can see the sweat slick on Bill's face and arms from the effort of working on the hedge. He is bare-chested under his overalls.

"I'll bring you some water," I say.

"Don't make yourself late for school," he says.

"I've got loads of time. I ran like a rabbit to get here."

Bill smiles at that. "All right then," he says. "A glass of water would be welcome."

Bill is nervous of the indoors. He doesn't like to be too long inside houses. It makes him feel trapped. He goes back to his clipping, and I walk up the path and into Mrs. Odegard's house. She always leaves the kitchen door unlocked. She must be resting upstairs, because she's not in the kitchen or the parlour. The pitcher of water is frosty from its spell in the icebox. I pour some into the largest glass I can find and take it outside to Bill. He downs the water in one swallow, wipes his mouth with the back of his hand, and passes the empty glass over to me. He's almost finished one side of the long hedge that grows between Mrs. Odegard's house and the street.

"I'll go and fetch you some more, Bill," I say, and just as I'm turning to head back towards the house, I hear a whistle and my body stiffens into place. I know that whistle, and it makes me afraid.

"Well, well," says a voice. "If it isn't crazy Bill and little Lenny."

It's Sam Munroe. He's walking along, smoking a cigarette, then crossing the street and coming towards us.

"*Rabbit Foot Bill from Sugar Hill. He never worked, and he never will.*"

"But he is working," I say, because it seems such a lie that Sam can chant that rhyme while Bill is so obviously cutting Mrs. Odegard's hedge.

"Shut up," says Sam. "I didn't say you could speak." He takes a pull on his cigarette and blows the smoke right into Bill's face.

Bill doesn't say anything, just looks square at Sam, and then plunges the shears hard into the boy's chest.

I hear the thud of metal hitting bone, and I see the shocked expression on Sam's face as he crumples to the ground. There's no blood until Bill reaches down and yanks the clippers out of the body, putting one foot on the boy's shoulder for leverage as he does this. Then the blood rivers out of Sam Munroe as fast as springtime.

Bill wipes the shears, slowly and deliberately, on the leg of his overalls and then, without saying a word, goes back to work clipping the hedge. The *snick snick* of the clippers is the only sound around me.

"Bill," I say. "Bill, I think he's dead. I think you've killed him."

Bill turns from his work, looks at me, and says, quite clearly, "He had it coming to him."

The trial is swift. The verdict certain. Bill makes no

effort to defend himself. I wait outside the courtroom on the day he is sentenced, and I watch him being led out of the building and into the police van. He is wearing leg irons—two cuffs of steel around his ankles and a short length of chain running between them. The irons look like the collar on the leghold trap I saw Bill set once for beaver.

I yell to him, but he's too far away to hear me.

What I never say to anyone is this: I didn't go for help. I stood there beside the hedge, a slow worm of satisfaction crawling through my blood, watching Snake die. I was glad Bill had stabbed him. It was the nicest thing anyone had ever done for me.

I don't know how I manage to find my way back to Sugar Hill, but I have remembered the way without even trying.

The door to Bill's house never closed properly. It doesn't have a latch, just notches into the dirt on either side of it, and when I walk up the path through the garden, I see that it's wide open.

The dogs have been at the rabbits. There are bones and bits of skin scattered across the earthen floor. There's a rabbit skull by the stove in the kitchen, one eye still socketed into the hollow of bone.

I stand in the middle of Bill's house and it suddenly seems small and squalid, like a pit dug into the earth, like a grave full of animal bones. When Bill was here it was huge. It was warm and cozy. Now I can feel the chill in the earth, and that cold also shrinks the place, makes it appear smaller.

Outside, the garden has been trampled by the dogs, or by the rabbits who must have grown suddenly bold with no one to shoot at them when they came to help themselves to the vegetables.

The dogs are long gone. They must have been more wild than Bill supposed and, after the rabbit carcasses were devoured, left in search of other food. They aren't waiting to be taken care of by me. They've gone off to look after themselves. Maybe they know that Bill isn't coming back. Maybe they knew before I did. Bill always said that dogs are smarter than people.

I climb up to the top of Sugar Hill and lie down in the vetch, as the dogs used to do. The clouds are low, flock across the sky above the hill. There's a fall of starlings, and a rise of heat crawling through the grass towards me. This is the last warm light of afternoon.

I am a boy. I am a dog. I am the rabbits with their hind feet gone. I am the climb and the drop, the flat land below the hill, the flat sky above. I am this place and the long walk towards it. I am everything he ever saw, everything he ever touched. I am all—I am only—him.

WEYBURN
MENTAL
HOSPITAL

—

SASKATCHEWAN
1959

HEAR THE SOUND OF CLASSICAL MUSIC BEFORE I open the door. Strings and the soft surge of orchestra—a soothing melody that stops me with a hand on the doorknob of the meeting room. I cock my head to one side and then to the other, like a bird, listening. I can hear no voices, just the strains of this gentle music.

When I open the door and enter the room, Dr. Christiansen and four of the other doctors are gathered in a circle of chairs at one end of the space. A small gramophone plays the music I heard from the hallway, and on a low table in the centre of the circle is a reel-to-reel tape recorder and six glasses of water.

The curtains are drawn tight against the windows of the meeting room, and it takes me a moment for my eyes to adjust to the dimness, after the brightness of the outdoors. I stumble as I walk across the carpet.

"Ah, Leonard," says Dr. Christiansen. "There you are, finally. Let me introduce you."

He waves his hand towards the circle of white-coated men.

"Carl Hepner. Daniel Mortimer. Ben Carter. William Scott."

"Dr. Leonard Flint," announces Dr. Christiansen, waving at me in turn.

None of the doctors say anything to me, but they all look hard in my direction. One of them nods at me. I have forgotten who he is already.

I take a seat in the empty chair beside William Scott, a diminutive black man with glasses, older than me, but not by much, and the only man whose name I have remembered because he was the last introduced.

"I'm sorry I'm late," I say. "It took me a while to find the room."

It had taken me a while to even find the building. Though I have been here for several days now, I hadn't fully realized how massive the hospital is. Mostly I've been in one small section of the compound. I hadn't known it would take me half an hour to even locate the right wing, let alone the meeting room itself. The scale of the complex is hard to adjust to—how the wings extend out from the central building like spokes in a wheel—and I am off in my perceptions, the way a drunk misjudges the distance between the car and the curb when exiting a taxi.

"I'll recap for you," says Dr. Christiansen helpfully. He raises an arm as though he's conducting the music that is slipping so gently through the gramophone speakers.

"Here at the Weyburn we believe that no one is sane and no one is mad. In order to help the people in our care, we need to understand what they're experiencing, understand their reality. We are undergoing a series of experiments here concerning a drug known as lysergic acid diethylamide, or LSD for short."

"What sort of experiments?" I ask.

"LSD, in its effects, mirrors the mind of a schizo-phrenic, so in order to better understand the sensations schizophrenics experience, we are taking the drug our-selves and recording the event."

I look at the tape recorder and then over at the record player. The soft, soothing background music, which first sounded so benign, is now beginning to unnerve me. But in the space where I'm listening to the music, the names of the doctors in the room suddenly come flooding in, and the order in which they were introduced.

"Music helps keep the drug experience a pleasant one," says Dr. Christiansen, following my gaze.

"LSD is also helpful with alcoholics," says Dr. Carter. "It often shows them the cause of their drinking by recreating early emotional states and experiences."

"Like time travel," says Dr. Christiansen.

"We're also thinking of using it in psychotherapy sessions," says Dr. Mortimer. "To be able to probe deeper into the subconscious."

"It's a consciousness-altering drug," explains Dr. Hepner.

"It creates an alternate reality," says Dr. Carter.

"Really, it's just a different perspective on this reality," continues Dr. Christiansen. "Altered perception. Don't worry, Dr. Flint."

My face must betray my nervousness.

"It's harmless. Completely harmless. And we take only a moderate amount of the drug ourselves."

He leans forward and picks up one of the water glasses from the table.

"It's administered as a liquid dose that has been mixed with water. Please, gentlemen." He gestures towards the table and the other doctors. They each take one of the glasses and I do the same.

"Bottoms up," says Dr. Christiansen, and we all drink and then set the empty glasses back down on the table.

"It will take about twenty minutes for the drug to take effect," says Dr. Scott to me. "Try to relax."

But I find it impossible to relax. I rub my sweaty palms on my thighs. My mouth feels dry, even though I have just drunk a full glass of water. The ticking of the clock on the wall behind Dr. Christiansen's head suddenly seems unnaturally loud. Is that the LSD taking effect, I wonder? I stare at my shoes, and the light brown carpet beneath them. Why had I agreed to be part of this experiment? Did I agree? When I took this job, I knew that there were medical experiments going on at the Weyburn Mental Hospital. The place had the reputation of being on the leading edge of mental health treatments. This is why I took the job, because it would be an exciting place to work. It hadn't occurred to me that the experiments weren't only performed on the patients, but on the doctors as well.

"What should I do?" I ask, full of panic.

"Just close your eyes and listen to the music," says Dr. Christiansen. He leans forward and snaps on the tape recorder.

"Session eight," he says. "Friday, August 14, 1959. Ten a.m. Participating doctors: Hepner, Mortimer, Carter, Scott, Flint, and myself." He stops. The other doctors all have their heads bowed as though they're in church and Dr. Christiansen is about to deliver the sermon.

"This is the first experience for Flint," continues Dr. Christiansen, "the third for Scott, and the fourth for Hepner, Mortimer, and Carter." He pauses. "For myself, this will be the sixteenth time under the influence of LSD."

The music plays cheerfully on in the background.

There's a long silence and then Dr. Hepner says, "That music is awfully pretty."

"Don't disappear into the music," says Dr. Christiansen. "Let it be background only. Try to stay present. Use it to guide you, but don't let it displace you or your thoughts."

There's another equally long silence, during which the ticking of the clock beats into my brain like a woodpecker hammering into a tree. I watch the minutes circle round and back again, round and back again. They climb up to the twelve, then swing down to the six. Is it my imagination, or does the climbing part seem slower than the falling part? Is the progress of time really this uneven, and why have I never noticed it before? Is the second hand of the clock weighted so that the ascent to noon and midnight is a labour and the drop to dawn and dinner a release?

"Carl," says Dr. Christiansen after a while, and then he says it again, very slowly and stretched out. "C-a-r-l. C-a-r-l. Your name seems to be growling at me. Can you make it stop?"

"I'm almost through the tunnels," says Dr. Hepner. "They are all different colours. Beautiful colours. There's red and purple and orange. I just went through a blue tunnel." He seems not to have heard what Dr. Christiansen has just said about him being a dog.

"What colour blue?" asks Dr. Christiansen, but I can still hear him saying, *Carl, Carl,* under his breath like an incantation.

"I think I might have achieved weightlessness," says Dr. Mortimer loudly. He jerks upwards, as though he's just woken up, or he's a marionette and someone is pulling on his strings.

"It's the same blue that's in the centre of a teardrop," continues Dr. Hepner. "Very beautiful. Like a sapphire."

"I don't feel anything at all," Dr. Scott whispers to me. "Do you?"

"No."

I hesitate for a moment.

"Although I don't know what I'm meant to be feeling, so it's a little confusing."

I watch the second hand on the clock strain upwards and fall back down. Then I watch a slit of light from between the curtains make a long mark, like a giant exclamation point, on the wall opposite. The long mark of light bends one way and then another. I think it must be the LSD causing that, until I can see that the window is open behind the curtain and it must be the breeze moving the curtains and altering the sliver of light.

"I suppose," says Dr. Scott after a moment, "the question becomes, where does their inner reality intersect with our outer reality?"

"What?"

"There's a border where they meet, but it can't be crossed over. There might even be a border guard in a little glass hut. And dogs. I'm pretty sure there is a fence with razor wire."

"What?" I say again.

"Have I stopped making sense?"

"Well, you make a certain kind of sense, but I don't think you're making 'normal' sense."

"Then the drug must be working after all." Dr. Scott leans back in his chair and closes his eyes.

The music dances on.

When I was in medical school, it seemed to me that the psychiatric residents were divided into the scientists and the doctors. The scientists were interested in discovering all the mysterious properties of the human brain. The doctors wanted to improve the lives of their patients. It appears that the doctors at the Weyburn are all scientists. I have mostly considered myself on the doctoring side of things. While I was drawn to an institution like the Weyburn when I graduated from medical school, drawn to the newness of its approach to mental illness, I'm not sure I am comfortable with what that newness might demand of me. I am, while not a cautious person exactly, someone who values routine. I like knowing what to expect from any given situation. The trouble with taking part in an experiment such as this one is that I will be placed into a situation over which I have no control, and that always makes me feel uneasy, and a little panicked.

Dr. Carter, who has been sitting quietly, watching the back of his hands, suddenly looks up and says, "There must be a million of them."

"A million what?" asks Dr. Christiansen.

Dr. Carter gazes at his hands again, reconsiders, and says, "There must be a million of them."

"The drug just seems to make our thoughts further away from us," I say to William Scott.

"What are you feeling?" he asks me.

"Nothing," I say.

But when I look down at my shoes again, the carpet is rising on either side of them, lapping at the edges of the leather. The more I stare at the carpet, the deeper into it I can see. There are currents and valleys. The individual fibres stand to attention like trees.

"I didn't realize the carpet was so alive," I say, but Dr. Scott no longer seems to be listening to me. He is humming and moving his body from side to side like a metronome.

"There must be a million of them," says Dr. Carter sadly, shaking his head. It seems like he might begin to cry.

From the corner of the room, there's a hissing as the gramophone needle reaches the end of the record.

"Can you see to that, Flint?" says Dr. Christiansen.

I have to move my shoes back through the forest in the carpet, back through the waves that lap at them, back into harbour. It takes enormous effort, but I somehow manage to do this, first one foot and then the other. Then I wobble to a standing position, go over to the gramophone, and put the needle back at the beginning of the record. The strings fill the room, and I feel better when I hear them start to play again.

THE DOCTORS AND some of the psychiatric nurses at the Weyburn are housed in cottages distant from and out of sight of the main hospital building. The wood-frame single-storey cottages are in a row, each about a hundred feet apart, and facing the river that runs through the hospital grounds. Most of the cottages are one-bedroom units, but there are several larger ones at the end of the row, designed for families. All of the doctors that were taking LSD with me in the meeting room live here on the hospital grounds. There are over 1,800 patients at the hospital at the moment, and staff is needed on site to manage them. The nurses and orderlies and office staff who don't live on the grounds of the hospital drive in from the nearby town. Dr. Christiansen has a large brick house there. It was pointed out to me on the drive to the Weyburn by the orderly who picked me up at the train station. It was a much grander affair than these modest frame buildings.

"It pays to be the big cheese," said the orderly.

My cottage has a bedroom, small sitting room with an old sofa and two chairs, galley kitchen, bathroom with only a shower stall, no tub, and a screened porch that overlooks the river.

The LSD experiments are a priority at the Weyburn, and on the mornings that the doctors take LSD, they are not expected to go back to work for the remainder of the day. It was hard enough for me to find the meeting room when I was sober, but reversing the process is even trickier. It takes me what seems like three months to walk back across the compound to my cottage, but when I get there, I find that only half an hour has elapsed. Time is proving to be a very confusing entity today.

I lie down on my bed, but closing my eyes makes me dizzy, so I stand up again. I pour myself a glass of water and take it out to the porch.

It's afternoon and the swallows arc and dive above the river in search of insects. Animal hunger always looks so graceful; human hunger rarely does. I watch the swoop and stall of the birds and drink the water. I feel tired and a bit dislocated, as though I have just completed a long train journey and can't yet reconcile where I have arrived with where I started. The shift from medical school to a real hospital feels like such a shock. Everything seemed easier in the abstract.

I concentrate on drinking and on watching the river in front of me. It is a modest river, not that wide, but it moves swiftly along. I can see the ripples of current on the surface, and I can smell the scent of the water—a rich, peaty odour from the sloughed-off bark and organic matter decaying on the riverbed. It is an old river, full of curves, the banks bulging out into small bays and then narrowing over a series of shallow rapids.

William Scott has the cottage next to mine on the right. He is also sitting out on his porch. I wave, but he doesn't appear to have seen me, just keeps staring ahead at the river. Probably he is doing the same thing that I am, trying to focus on what is right in front of him in an effort to recover from the lingering effects of the drug. Again, I think that the LSD, although taken in a group setting and meant to be interactive, has made us all more inward-looking.

I realize that I have gone from medical school, where I was part of a community that accepted me, where I had friends, to this place, where I am completely new and know no one, where I not only have no friends, but I can barely remember the names of my colleagues. It's a good thing my girlfriend, Amy, is coming here for the weekend. I am suddenly desperately lonely, and then immediately wonder if I am really having this feeling or if it's a result of taking the LSD.

Aside from settling into my cabin and having my information processed with the financial department, the drug experiment is the first real thing I have done in my new job at the Weyburn. It seems strange to do that before meeting any of my patients, but I realize that what is being demonstrated is the priority of the institution, or perhaps merely the priority of the leader of the hospital, Dr. Christiansen.

I sit out on the porch until I can see the first stars above the river. Then I feel hungry and tired, in quick succession, and go back indoors. After the laborious task of buttering a slice of bread, it seems somehow impossible to eat, so I just lie down on my bed and immediately fall into a deep, dreamless sleep.

DR. CHRISTIANSEN IS volunteering the better part of a week to show me around the Weyburn. It takes this long to cover all the many, and different, areas of the huge compound.

I have already seen the administrative offices and the fields that make up the massive farm. Now we are in the basement of the main hospital building, in a series of small, windowless cells with heating and water pipes running through them at head level.

"This is where they used to put the severely retarded patients," says Dr. Christiansen. "Back when they were called 'mental defectives.' Pitiful, isn't it?" He doesn't wait for my reply, strides on ahead through the dimly lit basement tunnels. "It's an outright travesty, the way some poor unfortunates were treated in the past," he says.

I admire his passionate outburst and remember the classifications from some of the older textbooks at medical school—"high-grade moron" for someone fairly functional, "moron" for someone less so, "imbecile" for a retardation level of medium grade, and "idiot" for a severely retarded person. This is how patients were categorized, and not too long ago, in the mental hospitals of the past. Back then they were kept together in one big room—women and men, violent and non-violent—no respect given for them being individuals, and no concern for their safety. One of the medical school doctors talked about these patients from the old hospitals being stripped naked and hosed down weekly, in lieu of being allowed to bathe themselves.

"Thank god for the reforms, sir," I say, struggling to keep pace with Dr. Christiansen as he strides ahead of me through the basement corridors.

"No need for that, Flint," he says. "We're both doctors here. You can call me Luke."

But I don't feel I can call him Luke. I am a freshly, barely qualified psychiatrist. He is older, more experienced, and the superintendent of this enormous facility of 1,800 patients and over 800 staff.

"There were no toilets down here," says Dr. Christiansen in disgust. "And no utensils for eating. The poor unfortunates had to mouth their food from bowls like dogs."

"That's terrible, sir," I say.

I feel lucky to have landed this job so soon out of school. The Weyburn is renowned for its liberal policies and radical treatments—the influence perhaps of the new socialist government of Saskatchewan. This new government is all about reforms. They have instituted the "rural electrification project" to bring electricity to the sixty thousand farms in the region that do without. They are also encouraging the emptying of the mental hospitals, retraining the patients to return to the outside world, reassimilating them back into the communities where they once belonged. The Weyburn might be full to bursting now with patients, but in a few years, it is hoped that it will be completely empty. The tasks that the patients are required to do while at the hospital—working on the hospital farm or in the mattress factory—will hopefully translate into skills they can use when they are reintroduced to the outside world.

"If you want to know the true history of a building," says Dr. Christiansen, "you go down or up. Down to the basement, up to the attic. That's where the secrets are."

I know I am supposed to be appalled at the conditions in the basement that the former patients suffered under, but I actually find the close, dark space rather comforting. The mental hospital has overwhelmed me. It is vast. When I came up the drive a few days ago, it felt as though I was entering another country. The driveway was flanked with trees, and it twisted and turned like the river. There is an entire working farm on the grounds with over 650 acres in cultivation and a full dairy herd. All the food for the hospital is produced there. The Weyburn is an entirely self-sustaining community. The hospital itself is the largest building in the entire province of Saskatchewan.

Dr. Christiansen leads me up a flight of stairs and along a hallway.

"We're much too overcrowded at the moment," he says, flinging open a door to a dormitory.

I look into the room he has opened. It is a flat field of beds. Each bed has a housecoat slung over the iron bedstead at the foot and a pair of slippers tucked under the middle of the bed, but there is no other personal space available. The beds are jammed together so tightly that to get to a bed on the far side of the room, one would have to walk across the other beds. There must be fifty beds in this room that is designed for perhaps twelve.

"It's a bit tight," I say.

"Can't be helped." Dr. Christiansen snaps the door shut and we continue along the corridor.

"Why are there so many patients?"

The Weyburn is the largest mental hospital in the country, but I can't believe that Saskatchewan has more mentally ill patients than elsewhere.

"In the '20s and '30s people were just sent here," says Dr. Christiansen. "Those who were mentally retarded or who were suffering from some sort of shock—women who were going through the change of life or who were depressed after childbirth. Anyone who behaved oddly, for any reason, could end up in the mental hospital."

"It was a dumping ground?"

"To be honest, yes." Dr. Christiansen runs a hand through his thinning hair. "Probably half of the patients weren't even mentally ill at all."

"So it might not be that hard to introduce them back into their communities?"

"Hopefully not."

My job, if I understand it correctly, is to help facilitate this. I am to be in charge of a hundred men. If they do not have work already in this hospital city, I am to find them some. Those that are working—on the farm, or in the mattress factory, or in the power plant—I am to help make the transition from their jobs at the hospital to equivalent jobs in the towns and villages outside the hospital. I am to be more of an employment counsellor than psychiatrist.

"I'm not sure how I will be at helping with this," I say. "It is a bit outside of my limited experience."

Dr. Christiansen stops in front of another door. He turns to face me, puts a hand on my shoulder.

"Leonard," he says, "why did you want to become a psychiatrist?"

"I want to help people who can't help themselves."

"Here we are helping people *to* help themselves." Dr. Christiansen pats me on the shoulder as one would pat the head of an obedient dog. "Which is actually a whole lot easier. You'll be fine." He opens the door of the room and I see forty or fifty grown men in various states of childlike behaviour. Some are on their knees on their beds, rocking, their heads bumping against the bed frames in a rhythmical tattoo, like a heartbeat. Some men are just sitting on the edges of their beds, staring into space or talking to themselves. One of the men is masturbating.

"This is the little boys' room," says Dr. Christiansen. "Nothing to be done for these men, I'm afraid. They won't be leaving here." He shuts the door crisply and we continue along the corridor.

The ward that I am to be in charge of consists of two dormitory rooms separated from each other by a sitting room and a kitchen, where the patients are expected to prepare their own breakfast before heading off to work for the day. Lunch is provided for them at their work stations, and dinner is served back here on the ward in the evening.

"Here it is," says Dr. Christiansen. "Your new domain." We are standing in the kitchen. He waves his arm towards the sitting room. "These men will become your new family. You will be their father."

"I will?"

I feel much too young to be a father, and especially to full-grown men who are all older than I am. I don't know what I imagined when I was in medical school, but it wasn't this. I was thinking more of one-to-one psychiatric sessions, of everything being measured and under my control, of grateful patients and my various brilliant diagnoses of their treatable conditions. I had imagined a safe, tidy office, with pictures of flowers or birds on the walls and comfortable chairs to sit in, perhaps a nice view out the window of trees and sky. The patients would enter individually, sit and talk for an hour, and then leave again. Several months, a year, and they would be cured of what had made them seek out treatment. I had not imagined the chaotic situation where I now find myself, but I had been persuaded into applying for this job by one of my teachers, who had convinced me that it would be a remarkable opportunity to work for an institution that was employing such innovative techniques to treat mental illness.

"I wish I'd had such opportunities when I was a young doctor," I remember him saying, and I was swayed by this because I know that my father felt regret for some parts of his life, and I don't want to feel regret for anything in mine.

But it all feels a bit overwhelming now that I am actually here and expected to do a job. I look around the kitchen and sitting area and try to imagine it filled with a hundred men, all looking to me for advice and guidance. How can I possibly be of assistance to a hundred men, all of whom have so much more life experience and so many more problems? I would have been better served going into dentistry. Looking into mouths all day would be better than this, and there would be regular hours, and perhaps the bright lights in the examination room would be cheering.

"Now we'll head to the gymnasium," says Dr. Christiansen, already back in the hallway. "I am particularly proud of our monthly dances and the patients' bowling league, and I want to show you where we keep the badminton nets and soccer balls."

AMY CALLS ME on Friday afternoon. I'm just about to leave my office to go back to the cottage to shower and shave in preparation for her arrival.

"I'm not coming," she says, her voice sounding irritable and close. "In fact, I haven't even left Montreal."

"What's wrong? Are you ill? Are your parents ill? Did you miss your train? Has it been delayed?"

"Leonard. Stop." She sighs into the receiver.

"Did you get my latest letter?" I ask. "I managed to get tickets to the theatre in Regina on Saturday night. And I booked us into a nice restaurant for dinner there. They have a dish called Steak Diane that is set on fire right at the table. It's supposed to be very impressive. And delicious."

"I'm not coming," says Amy flatly.

The phone receiver is slippery in my hand. I'm sweating and I can feel a bubble of nausea rising in my belly.

"Why not?"

She sighs again. "You try too hard," she says. "I can't keep pace with your letters. I'm always racing to catch up."

"But you don't need to keep pace."

"I feel that I do, that it's expected of me. You write to me every single day with all your thoughts and feelings."

"I want to share everything with you."

"Well," says Amy after a pause, "I don't actually require that much sharing."

"It was hard to get those theatre tickets," I say. "I was on the phone at first, but in the end I had to line up for them, and I was in that line for several hours. It was very hot out."

"Leonard, I'm sorry, but I'm breaking up with you."

"But why?"

"I just told you."

"I don't need to write you so many letters. I could

just send one a week. Sort of a compendium, with all my news condensed."

"If it wasn't letters, you'd be sending me flowers, or calling me on weeknights when I have to study. Or sending little gifts through the mail."

It seems absurd that Amy is complaining because I give her too much attention.

"My apartment is small," she says, sounding irritated again. "I don't have room for your little gifts."

"But I haven't sent any!"

"Goodbye, Leonard," she says. "I'm very sorry. Truly I am."

There's a click and then the long hum of the dial tone. I hold the receiver to my head and listen to it, hoping that Amy will see the error of her ways and pick up the phone again, reopen the line. But this doesn't happen.

DR. SCOTT IS swimming in the river when I return to my cottage. He waves at me.

"Join me, Leonard. The water is lovely at this time of day."

I haven't brought swim trunks with me to the Weyburn, because I wasn't really expecting the river, so I strip down to my boxers and jump in. I want to descend to the depths, my terrible sadness making it impossible for me to ever surface again. Amy would have to be devastated if I drowned. But the river isn't very deep at all. I can touch bottom immediately.

Dr. Scott and I breaststroke up to the willow tree at the bend in the river and then back again. Despite myself, the water feels good against my skin, and the sensation of weightlessness lifts some of my sorrow. It also makes me think of Dr. Mortimer's comment during the LSD session last week.

"Was that really only your third drug experiment?" I ask Dr. Scott.

"I've only been here for four months," he says. "Next to you, I'm the most recent hire. I had the flu at one of the sessions and opted out." We breaststroke past a patch of lily pads. "They're a monthly occurrence."

"Every month?"

"Yes. Mandatory. First Monday of every month." William Scott looks over at me. "Isn't that why you took this job? It's why I took it. I have a personal interest in emancipation—my mother was descended from slaves—and I find the idea of freeing these patients thrilling. Thrilling because we will be able to free them both in body and mind."

"Honestly," I say, "I took the job because I'm from Saskatchewan and I didn't really like Montreal, where I was living after medical school, so I thought it would be good to come back to my home province."

"It wasn't because of the reforms?"

"I didn't give them a second thought."

Dr. Scott laughs. "Dr. Christiansen called you a keen new recruit," he says. "He was very excited to have you on board."

"Well, I'm not unkeen," I say.

We swim past my cottage. Then past William Scott's cottage.

"If you're worried about the LSD sessions, it's less odd when you are using the drug alongside the patients," says Dr. Scott. "Then you can harness it to a purpose and it makes more sense, feels more controllable."

We have reached the willow tree. The fronds swing down almost to the water and remind me of Amy's hair, lifting in the breeze from her apartment window when she sat working at her desk. I remember the phone call and start to feel ill again.

"My girlfriend broke up with me," I say. "Today. She was meant to be coming here this weekend. She lives in Montreal."

"Ah." William Scott executes a smooth turn and we begin swimming upriver again. "Because of the distance?"

I can see that this is the logical answer and that it is best to fasten myself to it going forward.

"Yes," I say. "It was because of the distance."

The swimming makes me feel better, and also the company of Dr. Scott. But when we climb out of the river and head into our respective cottages, I sink into gloom again. After drying off and donning clothes, I pace around my small living room, but I can't settle, so I head back to the hospital, into my office there, and dial Amy's number.

"Hello," she says, sounding weary as she answers the phone, which makes me think that she has been waiting for me to call back and this weariness is because I have proved her right in doing so.

"Is there someone else?"

"What?" There's a pause. "Leonard, is that you?"

"Is there someone else?" I say again. "Are you seeing someone in Montreal? Do you have another boyfriend? Have you been cheating on me?"

Because it feels better to me if Amy has another lover rather than just ending things because she doesn't like me enough. Having it be about someone else is not as bad as having it be solely about my being a disappointment to her.

"No. There isn't anyone else."

"Are you sure?"

"What kind of question is that? Of course I'm sure." Amy sighs into the receiver. "Leonard, you are being ridiculous. Why can't you just accept that I don't want to be with you?"

"Because it's a very hard thing to accept, Amy."

"Well, get used to it."

She hangs up on me.

I call back, but she doesn't pick up. I sit at my desk, holding the phone receiver in my hand, trying to believe that it's really over, but the sad truth of it is that since Amy broke up with me, I love her more than ever.

MY FIRST MORNING on my ward, I mean to wake early enough to have breakfast with the men in my charge, but I sleep through my alarm, and by the time I have run across the field between the cottages and the hospital, most of my patients have left already for their day's work. The ones who are still there, washing dishes and wiping down the tables, eye me suspiciously when I burst through the sitting room doors, out of breath and panic-stricken.

I had meant to give a little speech to the assembled men, introduce myself, and let them know I will make myself available to them, but there is no point when so few remain on the ward. I will have to wait for dinner, when they'll be back here again. In the meantime I will busy myself with reading their files, try to learn their names and histories.

My office is at the end of the ward, a pleasant square cinder-block room with a window that overlooks the laundry building. I have the duty nurse retrieve the relevant documents for me and I fetch myself a cup of coffee from the staff lounge. Then I settle down to a day's work of perusing the case files of the hundred men in my sudden, and so far hapless, care.

It is as I thought, in that most of the men in my charge are older than me. Many are alcoholic. Some are schizophrenic, some depressive. There is one pyromaniac, named Henry Tudor, who has been sent to work in the mattress factory. Putting an arsonist in a building full of flammable materials would not be my first choice, but I can also see the strange logic in it. After all, if Henry wants to start a fire, he will start it no matter where he is. Why not put him in the path of temptation? This would be a way to cure him of his fiery impulses.

Many of the men were sent to the mental hospital by their families, some were former wards of the state, and a few men were actually born in the mental hospital. Their files have the word *institutionalized* written inside the box for listing the particulars of their disease. These men have never known anything but this place, and even though they are being trained to be functional in the outside world, how will they survive the chaos and unpredictability of normal life? How will they be able to comprehend it? Are people really versatile enough to deal with such radical change in their lives—especially those who have had to cope with such extremes of experience?

I remember Dr. Christiansen telling me on the hospital tour that babies born at a mental hospital are sent immediately to a regular hospital so as not to have *born at the mental hospital* written on their birth certificate. Most of these babies will have nothing wrong with them in a psychiatric sense, but growing up on the ward, in the company of mentally ill adults, will force a kind of mental illness on them and they will have difficulty adapting to what we think of as "regular life." Finding a place for these patients outside of the institution will be a much harder task than finding placements for those men who have some experience of the world outside of the hospital walls, and who remember what it was like to belong to that other life.

I feel less overwhelmed as I read the case files. The more I learn about the men, the less alarming they seem. I can find commonalities with them as individuals, and they don't seem as frightening as they were before I knew anything about them. At medical school I excelled at diagnosing, at compressing relevant patient information into a condition with a treatable outcome.

Several of the alcoholic patients have notes tucked into their files that read, *Selected for behavioural modification experiments.* The notes bear the signature of Luke Christiansen. This must mean they are targeted to undergo LSD treatment. I remember Dr. Christiansen saying that the therapy worked particularly well on alcoholic patients.

At lunchtime one of the duty nurses brings me a tray of food—pea soup, cold beef sandwich, dish of custard, another cup of coffee. It's not bad and I finish all of it, reading the files while I eat, careful not to smear my lunch over the crisp white typewritten pages that summarize each man.

When I began reading the files, the individuality of the patients stood out for me, but by the end of the day, I have read through so many files that the particulars of the patients swim together into a mass of indistinguishable detail. Which man was sent here with his sister? Which man has uncontrollable rages?

When I arrive that evening, I find that I don't need to announce myself to the men. My white coat does this for me.

"Look, it's the new doctor," someone shouts as I enter the kitchen, and everyone seems to turn and stare at me as I walk across the floor and take a seat at one of the long tables by the window.

"Doc," says the man opposite me, "I need stronger pain medication for the arthritis in my knees."

"I'm waiting for a package," says another man. "I don't know why it hasn't come."

"My mother hasn't come," says someone else.

The air is full of complaints and requests. In a moment of sudden inspiration, I take my notepad and a pen from the breast pocket of my coat and I pass these to the man on my left.

"Write down your request," I say, "and put your

name beside it, and I will deal with each man's problem in turn."

DR. CHRISTIANSEN CALLS me into his office as I'm walking past on the way back to my cottage after dinner.

"Flint!"

I step inside, fearful he is going to call me out for some mistake I have undoubtedly made at supper.

"Close the door." He waves his hand towards the empty chair in front of his desk. "And have a seat."

I do as he says.

"Flint, I would like you to do me a favour."

The relief flooding through me is intense.

"Of course, sir."

"I have managed to persuade my wife, Agatha, to help with the dance this Friday. It took some doing to persuade her." Dr. Christiansen taps a cigarette on the front of his silver case and lights it. "She's not exactly fitting in here. I mean, she's not very happy with life in Saskatchewan." He takes a deep draw on his cigarette and blows the smoke towards me. "Understandable really."

"Why?" I move my head to avoid getting asphyxiated.

"She misses our children."

"They didn't come with you?"

"No, they're back in England. At boarding school."

Luke Christiansen taps the ash from his cigarette into a crude dish shaped like a palm tree and painted a lurid green. He sees me looking at it.

"We had a pottery program here once," he says. "Quite successful for a while, but then there were several instances of patients eating the clay." He sighs. "The dances are a much better fit. Anyway, where was I? Oh yes, Agatha isn't very happy here. She doesn't seem to like any of the other doctors. But you are younger and, if you don't mind me saying so, not very doctor-like yet, so she might feel differently." Dr. Christiansen leans across the desk towards me. I can smell the smoke and spicy cologne on his skin and I can see the little coin of baldness on the top of his head.

"We are doing very important work here, Flint," says Dr. Christiansen. "Very important work. I need for everything to run smoothly. And so I need Agatha to be happier."

I'm not sure what any of this has to do with me.

"What can I do to help?" I ask.

"Befriend her. Be a sympathetic ear. Assist her with the preparations for the dance. She's putting up decorations this moment, I think. In the gymnasium."

I recognize an order when I hear one.

"Yes, sir."

"Good man." Dr. Christiansen gets up to open the door for me. "And much appreciated."

⌣

AGATHA CHRISTIANSEN IS standing on a stepladder looping a length of yellow crepe paper streamer along one wall of the gymnasium. Like her husband, she smokes, has a cigarette hanging from the corner of her mouth. She looks down at the sound of the heavy wooden doors closing behind me.

"I suppose Luke sent you?"

I walk across the gym floor towards her. There seems no point in lying.

"Yes."

"That bastard," she says, turning her attention back to the length of yellow streamer. "But I admit I could do with some assistance. These damn things keep catching on fire."

There are ashes on the floor beneath the ladder, a strip of charred streamer hanging limply from one of the rungs.

"Maybe you should put out your cigarette."

"Maybe I should." Agatha comes down two steps on the ladder, looks hard at me. "How old are you? Twelve?"

"Twenty-four."

"Not really old enough for anything," she says.

"Old enough to be a doctor here at the Weyburn."

She smiles at that, descends the last steps of the ladder so that she is standing in front of me. We are the same height. "You're a scrappy one," she says. "Luke usually prefers his followers to be more docile." She takes the cigarette from her mouth, taps the long ash onto the wooden floor between us. "Handsome too. I bet the girls are crazy for you."

This makes me remember Amy, the recent, terrible phone call, and my fruitless attempts to have her listen to reason. (I have tried to call her back several times since she broke up with me, and she has hung up on me each and every time, unwilling to listen to any of my heartfelt pleas for reconsideration and my declarations of love.)

"Not really," I say. "I did have a girlfriend, but she lives in Montreal and we couldn't stay together." I pause. "On account of the distance."

"Really?" Agatha tilts her head at me, the expression on her face one of skepticism. "In my experience, distance is very attractive. Makes the heart grow fonder. Lends enchantment. That sort of thing."

"She was tired of my letters," I admit. "I sent too many and overburdened her. She said I tried too hard."

Agatha Christiansen snorts with laughter.

"Little idiot," she says.

At first I think she means me, and I stiffen in indignation. But she leans over and brushes something from my shoulder, the gesture light and tender, and then I know that she is talking about Amy.

⁓

THE DANCES AT the Weyburn are very popular—much more popular than the pottery program would have been, even if people weren't eating the clay. Physical activity is always more stimulating than something static like arts and crafts. Better to run after a ball or swing a racquet than paint a night sky full of clumsy stars or make skinny animals out of pipe cleaners.

At dinner before the dance on Friday, the men on my ward are buzzing with excitement.

"It's best when there's a live band," one of them says. "And worst when the band is made up of people from here, because no one is any good."

"A dead band," offers another man. (I am struggling to learn their names and having no luck, but at least they are beginning to look familiar.)

"Remember when someone drowned in the well after that dance last year?" a third man says. "It was an awful mess fishing him out."

"They didn't find him until weeks later," explains someone else.

I am getting used to these dinner conversations, how topics slide with alarming rapidity from one topic to another and often end with death. It's a kind of short-hand that families use. No need to explain everything when the participants know one another so well. The men on this ward, on each ward of the hospital, have been together for years and have an intimacy that speaks to that.

At the dance the music plays through a gramophone, with two of the patients controlling the placement of the records on the turntable—one to snatch the record off and the other to put the new one down.

"Not a fool-proof method," says William Scott, who has come to stand beside me against the wall. "I'm told there have been fist fights if one of them does their part too slowly."

There are punch bowls and two kinds of cookies, and the streamers hanging from the ceiling are only slightly lopsided.

I dance with one of the nurses and several of the female patients. No one, including myself, is a very good dancer, but what we all lack in skill, we make up for in exuberance. I find that I am enjoying myself more than I thought I would. It is good to stop worrying about what kind of job I am doing and just move my feet in time with the music.

When I take a break from dancing to catch my breath, I notice Agatha Christiansen standing near one of the punch stations. We lock eyes and she saunters over to me.

"Shall we?" She holds out her hand.

We dance close, her arms wrapped around my neck.

Her hair reeks of smoke and hairspray. I can smell alcohol on her breath.

"You know," she whispers in my ear, "you can try hard with me any time you want."

Her blatant proposition shocks me, and I don't know what to say in response.

I can see Dr. Christiansen over her shoulder, dancing with one of the female patients, laughing as he twirls her around and she ducks under his outstretched arm.

I pull away from Mrs. Christiansen.

"Sorry," I say, "but I have to go now."

I flee into the hallway and then out of the building into the night. I have forgotten to bring a flashlight with me and the lights around the hospital building wash out after a few hundred feet into darkness. After that there's only the waning moon to show my way.

The main hospital path leaves the front entrance, passes by some of the farm buildings, and then winds along the river to the cottages. The cottages are probably a mile distant from the hospital, the farthest buildings from the main compound. I suppose this is meant to ensure we have some measure of privacy, but now the distance feels excessive.

I'm passing the stables, where the working team of horses, the Percherons, are housed, when I see the man. He's moving along the outside of the building. He's far enough away to be in the shadows and he has his back to me, but I recognize the way he moves as though it was myself moving in my own skin. I rush from the path towards the barn, but by the time I get there, the man who I swear is Rabbit Foot Bill, has disappeared.

When I get back to the cottage, I can't quiet myself. I lie in bed. I get up and pace around the room. I make some tea. I walk outside and stand by the river. I go back indoors. I sit in a chair. I lie down in the bed again.

When I was twelve they took Bill away to the Prince Albert Penitentiary because there was not a hospital for the criminally insane. I have never been to the prison, but I know that it is a hard place, a severe place. This mental hospital is a resort in comparison. The inmates there would not have the freedoms of this institution. The prison is not a place for rehabilitation. It is penitential, with cells and punishments. But if one was a good prisoner there, followed the rules and didn't cause any trouble, then perhaps they might be transferred to a place such as this? Is that how Bill got here?

It is half my life ago, but I can remember Bill and my time with him as though no years have passed at all. I can feel it in my body, the pull of wanting to be near him, and I realize, with a shock, that nothing has altered with my becoming an adult, that I still love him as much as I ever did.

~

IN THE MORNING I search out Dr. Christiansen in his office.

"I was wondering," I say, "if there's a patient at this hospital by the name of William Dunn?"

"Dunn?" Dr. Christiansen gets up and goes over to the filing cabinet near the window. He opens the top drawer and rifles through the folders. "One of your patients?" he asks.

"No, not a patient of mine. But he's from the same small town as I am. I used to know him there and I thought I saw him yesterday here, out near the barn."

"Dunn. William. Yes, here it is." Dr. Christiansen extracts a file from the cabinet and brings it over to his desk. He opens it.

"He was transferred here from the Prince Albert Penitentiary two years ago. We have him working with the horses. He's good with animals, seems to have a knack. That's strange." Dr. Christiansen looks up at me. "It seems we allow him to sleep in the stables instead of on the ward."

"He always preferred animals to people," I say. "And he had trouble being indoors."

"He may sleep in the stables," says Dr. Christiansen, "but technically he is on a ward and has a doctor in charge of him. I'm afraid it's not your ward, Flint," he says, shutting the file. "And you're not his doctor. It might upset him to see someone from his past. He's not schizophrenic, but he displays periodic bouts of psychotic behaviour. It's probably best if you don't renew your acquaintance with this William Dunn."

I RUN OUT to the stables as hard and fast as I can, my white doctor's coat flapping behind me like a sail.

It's dark inside the building and it takes a moment for my eyes to adjust to the change in light. I stand just beyond the doors, panting. I can hear the whicker of a horse and the rasp of my own breathing, and then I can see him, can see Bill. He's standing outside the row of stalls, a bucket in one hand, a length of rope in the other. He looks taller and leaner, but otherwise recognizably the same. The same thick black hair. The same long limbs.

"Bill," I shout across the warm darkness of the barn. "Bill, it's me. It's Lenny."

He comes towards me then, bucket and rope still in hand, until he's standing right in front of me. His face is more deeply lined and his eyes have a flicker of fear or nervousness in them that they didn't possess before, but he's still the same man I remember from when I was a boy. I feel flooded with happiness.

"Doctor," he says, "what did I do?"

"No, Bill, it's me. It's Lenny. From Canwood. From when you lived in Sugar Hill. Remember?"

He peers at me, even though we're standing inches away from each other. He looks deep into my face, his forehead tightened into a frown.

"I don't know you, doctor."

"Because I wasn't a doctor then. I was a boy. I was a twelve-year-old boy when you last saw me. I don't look exactly the same."

I want to say, *When you last saw me was when you killed Sam Munroe, when they took you away, when you were called Rabbit Foot Bill,* but I don't want to upset him with unpleasant associations of the past.

"I used to come and see you in your house in Sugar Hill."

"How did you know I lived in Sugar Hill?"

"Because I would visit you there."

"You would?"

"You often did work for Mrs. Odegard and I would visit you there too. Remember, you used to cut her hedge."

Bill considers for a moment. "Yes," he says after a while. "I recollect I did cut a hedge."

"Don't you remember me, Bill?"

I know he probably underwent all sorts of punishments when he was in prison. He might have been tortured by guards or by the other prisoners. Or sent to rot in solitary confinement. He's sure to have suffered from various deprivations, and maybe this is why he can't seem to make the leap from the image of the boy I was to the image of the man I have become. I have changed but surely not completely? It breaks my heart that he doesn't recognize me.

"No." Bill shakes his head slowly. "I don't believe I do know you."

"Well, I'll try to help you remember."

"All right, Dr. Lenny," says Bill agreeably. "If that's what you want to do."

That's what's different about him, a passivity that wasn't there when he was a free man. Most likely this is the result of years of institutional living. I hate to think that he's been broken, that his spirit is damaged, but I also have to accept that twelve years of captivity will change any man.

"You live here now?" I ask. "In the stable?"

Bill nods.

I notice that the bucket he's carrying is full of water. "That bucket must be heavy," I say. "Put it down for a moment and show me where you live."

Bill obediently places the bucket on the floor of the stable and leads me back past the row of stalls to the last enclosure on the left-hand side. He pushes open the swinging half door and I see the cot, bedding neatly made, and the small table beside it with a flashlight and a cup on it. The rest of the stall is empty—empty and very clean.

"There's more room here than on the ward," I say, and Bill nods again.

"I couldn't abide it there," he says. "There were too many people. They made too many noises."

"Don't the horses make noise?" I look down the row of stalls, at the heads of the horses all turned towards us, watching curiously.

"I know what the horse noises mean," says Bill. "People sometimes make noises that have no sense to them."

I have an overwhelming desire to throw myself down on Bill's bed, the way I would throw myself onto the fur-covered hay bales in his house on Sugar Hill.

"Do you miss Canwood?" I ask. "Do you miss Sugar Hill?"

Bill shifts from side to side, as though it makes him uncomfortable to think back to the town and his home. Perhaps it upsets him too much to remember anything around the murder and that is why he has blocked out the memory of me also.

"I like it here," he says.

"What do you like?"

"The horses."

"What about the hospital?"

"I don't go into the hospital, unless a doctor comes out here and tells me to." Bill reaches out and touches my shoulder. "That's what I thought you were here to do, Dr. Lenny—make me come back with you to the hospital. You have the look of a doctor."

"I am a doctor," I say, "but I haven't come to make you do anything. I just wanted to see you, Bill."

"Because you know me?"

"Yes." I like the heaviness of Bill's hand on my shoulder. It feels exactly like I remember. "And because you know me."

I DO WORRY about going so directly against Dr. Christiansen's orders, but when I walk away from my visit with Bill in the stables, I feel almost giddy with happiness, and that feeling overrides any trace of guilt. It is all right that Bill does not remember me. I will get to know him all over again and then, when he feels comfortable with me, he'll be able to recall my younger self. There are so many questions I want to ask him, but first I have to make him trust me again, trust me as he did when I was a boy.

Back at the cottage I rummage around in the bureau until I find what I'm looking for—the six rabbits' feet I collected from Bill when I was twelve. I lay them out on the top of the bureau, in order of size, just as I used to. If I push down hard on the top of the feet, their toes will make little holes in the wooden surface of the dresser.

I have learned some things about rabbits' feet in the years before meeting up with Bill again. I made it my business to learn. I know that to be truly lucky, a rabbit's foot should be cut from a living rabbit at the time of a new moon. The rabbit should be caught in a cemetery. This is because some folklorists believe that the rabbit is actually a shape-shifted witch and to cut the feet off the rabbit is to disable the powers of the witch.

The foot is thought to be able to ward off evil because a rabbit's powerful hind legs touch down on the earth before their front legs do, and the strength of this action can ward off spirits from the underworld.

More benign associations have the rabbit's foot as lucky because rabbits are connected with spring and the return of flowers, the return of life. To see a rabbit running across your land meant that you would enjoy a fertile garden that year, or that it would be a good time to set about having children.

I especially like the superstition that states that it is only good luck to carry a rabbit's foot if that foot has been given to you as a gift. If the killer of the rabbit keeps the foot for himself, it will only bring misfortune.

There's a sudden, sharp knocking at the front door. I walk across the room to answer it. Agatha Christiansen stands on the porch.

"I've come to apologize," she says through the screen. "I didn't mean to frighten you."

"You didn't frighten me."

"Didn't I?"

"Not at all."

She tilts her head to one side, a gesture I now recognize as belonging to her. "Then why haven't you invited me in?"

I open the screen door, wordlessly, and she steps into the cottage.

"I like what you've done with the place," she says, and that makes me smile.

"Thank you."

We stand opposite each other. She smiles at me and I see how beautiful she is. Her eyes are the colour of sunlit wheat.

I feel emboldened from having seen Bill, and full of happiness, and maybe this is why it is the simplest thing in the world to lean in and kiss Agatha Christiansen as she stands in the little galley kitchen.

"Well, well," she says after we break apart. "You are full of surprises." She takes my hand and leads me into the bedroom.

Sex with Agatha is nothing like sex with Amy, who gave out her passion in small, measured increments and then seemed to immediately resent it. Agatha laughs inappropriately, bites my shoulder so hard that she draws blood, cries when she comes, her tears hot stars blooming on my skin.

I can't get enough of her. But after a couple of hours, she dresses, fixes her hair in the tiny bathroom mirror, reapplies her lipstick.

"Not a word to anyone," she says. "I was never here."

"Of course."

I hand over her shoes, one at a time, watch as she slips them on. "But I will see you again, won't I?"

"Absolutely." Agatha lays a hand against my cheek and I close my eyes to feel the touch more intensely. "Whenever it is possible I will come here, to you. But no one must find out. And you must never come to me. Understood? We have to be discreet."

"I have as much to lose as you do," I say. "You can trust me."

"Yes." Agatha gives my cheek a little pinch. "I believe that I can."

I decide to go for a swim after she leaves, to help wash away the terrible guilt I suddenly feel for sleeping with the wife of my new boss.

The river is peaty, and a little metallic. It smells old and earthy, full of sloughed-off bark and wet stones. It is warmer than I expect, and when I slide off the bank, I am surprised at how good the water feels. It is as warm as bath water, but softer. I like being eye level with the sticks and leaves floating on the surface. I like the tangle of alders along the banks and the darkening sky above the trees.

I put my feet down. The bottom of the river seems to be cluttered with rocks and logs. I touch the smooth shape of stones, the slimy decay of wood. In some spots the water is only up to my waist, and then I move a few feet to the left and the water is over my head.

The river is a path cut between the fields. The current is strong enough that I can just lie on my back and float. I am a dark boat cast down the dark length of the river.

I mean to go to see Bill before supper, but I swim for too long, drifting languorously downriver, remembering how Agatha's body felt under mine, and letting my guilt slip away from me slowly. By the time I'm dressed again, it's too late to stop at the stables on my way to the ward.

It's hard to reconcile the distance between the cottages and the hospital. I'm always underestimating the time it takes for me to go between one place and the other.

The air is soft and the sun has turned everything golden. I hurry past the stables and imagine Bill in there, sitting on the edge of his cot, in his stall, eating the tray of food that someone has presumably brought out to him. I remember him as a fast eater, bolting his food like a dog. He will eat and then wipe his mouth with the back of his hand, gulp a glass of water, and then stand, rub his hands on the legs of his trousers, and return to his work without a word. He was never one to linger over meals. Food was simply an interruption to work. There was no real pleasure in it.

I should rotate where I sit every evening at dinner, move among the men so I get the chance to talk to all of them, to know them; but when I enter the ward kitchen, the men have left the space free where I had been sitting the previous night, and so I just sit back in the same place as last night, and beside the same people.

Supper is spaghetti and meat sauce, with bread in baskets on the table and apple pie for dessert. The bread is not as good as the bread Bill used to make in his outdoor oven. It is white and full of air and the crusts are stale and it seems like it might have been baked a few days ago, rather than having been made fresh for tonight's supper.

"Doc," says the man next to me, "did you see about my package yet?"

"I'm looking into it," I say, but I realize that I haven't even opened the notebook where I had the men write down their complaints and requests. Tomorrow, I think, wiping my plate around with the substandard bread because I'm hungry after swimming in the river and making love to Agatha. Tomorrow I will do a better job at my job.

I became a psychiatrist because of Rabbit Foot Bill, because I could never shake the sight of him being taken away at the end of his trial. He was adept at living how he lived, but he couldn't cope with the ordinary ways of society, and because I couldn't help him with this when

I was a boy, when I grew up I wanted to be able to help others like him.

This is what I had told myself all the way through medical school. But perhaps I was wrong. Perhaps it wasn't that I wanted to help a legion of unknown people, but that I only really ever wanted to help Bill. It was easy to pretend otherwise when he had disappeared out of my life. Now that he's back in proximity to me, I am no longer interested in the welfare of anyone else. It takes all my strength to remain seated in the ward kitchen, finishing my supper, making polite conversation with the men around me, and not be rushing out to the stables to eat with Bill.

THE NEXT MORNING I wake up determined to prove myself wrong, determined to better serve the men who have been entrusted to my care. I will do this by systematically visiting them where they work. I can get to know them in an active setting and on an individual basis, rather than in the passive, group setting of the ward.

I begin with the mattress factory and Henry Tudor. From the files I know that Henry Tudor was the victim of a house fire when he was young. The fire killed his family, and not only did he never recover from this loss, but he grew up to become a pyromaniac, setting a series of fires in the ramshackle garages and sheds in the west end of the city. It's unclear from his file whether he was the one who set the original fire, the one that killed his mother and father and baby brother.

Like Bill, Henry Tudor was first sent to the penitentiary and then moved here to the mental hospital. Now he works in the mattress factory, a low brick building opposite the farm. There, all the mattresses for the hospital are made and repaired. There are sewing machines and bolts of fabric for the mattress covers, bundles of batting, all jammed into a space that is not much bigger than a dormitory on the wards.

I ask the supervisor for Henry Tudor and he points to the back of the room. I see a middle-aged man shuffling towards me with an armful of mattress batting. He shuffles forward and then he seems to shuffle back, and then he shuffles forward again.

"What's he doing?" I ask the supervisor.

"That's the way he moves," he says. "Three steps forward, two steps back. He's slow, but he gets where he's going in the end. Here in the shop we call him Two Step."

I walk towards Henry Tudor, and when I get close I can hear that he's saying something under his breath as he shuffles forward and then back again.

"Burn their heads, burn their bodies, burn their bones," he says, the rhythmical incantation driving the movement of his feet, or the other way around. I cannot tell. "Burn their heads, burn their bodies, burn their bones."

"Hello, Henry," I say, but he keeps his head bowed, keeps muttering his line of words, keeps shuffling his way towards the front of the room.

"Henry." I grab his arm to stop his forward movement, to make him acknowledge me.

He looks up with panic in his eyes, and I realize my mistake in touching him.

"Burn their heads, burn their bodies, burn their bones," he says loudly, as though the words have become a spell to ward me off. "Burn their heads, burn their bodies, burn their bones." He's shouting now and the other workers in the factory have looked up from their tasks and are watching us. I let go of his arm.

"It's okay," I say. "It's okay. I just wanted to say hello. I don't mean you any harm."

Henry has his head bowed again and the line of words is being spoken at a softer volume. He resumes his strange halting walk as though I'm not there at all, and so I retreat back to the supervisor.

"I didn't mean to upset him," I say. "He's on my ward. I just wanted to make contact with him."

"Henry's not really one for contact," says the supervisor. He has a smirk on his face. "I could have told you that, if you'd asked."

Again I feel that I have made another mistake, that, for all my good intentions, I am botching this job at every opportunity. Every time I reach out, something goes wrong.

"I'll just stand here and watch him for a while," I say.

"Yes," says the supervisor, a man almost as young as I am. "You can't come to any harm doing that."

Henry Tudor, in his slow, uneven walk, brings his armload of batting up to a workbench where a mattress lies. The cover of the mattress is open down one side and Henry begins to stuff the mattress with the batting. Not only does he have trouble walking, but his hands appear to have tremors and the stuffing of the mattress is a long, rather painful process.

"Do you think he'll ever be fit to leave here?" I ask the supervisor.

"Henry? No, he won't be getting out. But the others"—the supervisor waves his hand over the rest of the roomful of men—"they'll be going. We've already placed one so far. George Ferguson. He left last week, went to work in a feed store."

"How's he doing?"

"Fine." The supervisor grins at me. "They're not going off to be bank presidents," he says. "Mostly they're pushing brooms or fetching and carrying." He taps his temple with an index finger. "Nothing too taxing," he says. "If you know what I mean."

I find his behaviour insulting, but I can't complain about it, seeing how he is succeeding here, whereas I am failing in my pitiful attempt to befriend Henry Tudor.

"Is he happy?" I ask.

"Who?"

"George Ferguson."

The supervisor gives me a strange look. "What kind of a question is that?" he says.

I GO TO visit Tom Bright in the garden. He's tying up the runner beans that are almost ready to harvest. He's an old man, with a thatch of white hair and dungarees that are too big for him and are held up by homemade suspenders that seem to have been fashioned out of two dog leads.

"Those are nice-looking beans," I say.

"You know something of beans, then?" says Tom.

"Not really." I follow him down the row. He has a ball of string tucked into his pocket, cuts off lengths with a penknife he holds in his right hand.

"They just look like good beans," I say. "Healthy beans. Tasty beans."

Tom snorts. "Why would you say a thing you don't mean?" he asks.

"I do mean it."

"You just said you know nothing of beans."

I decide to try a different approach. "Can I help you with this?"

I reach for his ball of string, and he snatches it out of my reach.

"No, I have a system."

"I see that. It looks like a good system."

"You know nothing of my system," says Tom Bright. Another change of direction is called for.

"Are you hoping to find work as a gardener when you leave the hospital? Do you need me to search out possible jobs for you?"

"I like it here," says Tom Bright. "This is my garden. These are my beans. I don't like any interference while I'm about my work."

He pushes past me to finish tying the row.

MARCUS STEUBING SWEEPS up hair in the barbershop. He scuffs the broom across the floor, pushing the locks into a dustpan, and empties the dustpan into a large metal garbage bin in the corner of the room. Then he comes back and repeats the task.

"Do you like your job?" I ask, following him to the garbage bin.

"No, I hate it."

"Would you like me to find you something else then?"

"No."

"Why not?"

"I'd hate it." Marcus Steubing leans on his broom and looks hard at me. "I hate this whole friggin' place. I'm being kept here against my will."

"But the hospital is being emptied," I say. "I don't think anyone wants to keep you here against your will. No one wants to keep you here at all. I can work at getting you a job outside of the hospital."

"Others have tried," says Marcus darkly. "Others have failed."

He knocks the broom against my shoes.

"You're in my way," he says. "You need to move."

I skitter a few feet to the left.

"Do you like hair, then?" I ask.

"What kind of a question is that?" Marcus regards me suspiciously.

"I mean, I could look for work for you at a wig-maker's or in a barbershop in town."

"I'd hate that. I hate hair."

"But you're doing this job, sweeping up hair?"

"I have to do something, don't I," says Marcus. "They make me do something." He mumbles something under his breath.

"Pardon?"

"It's all against my will," he says. "Including this conversation."

BRIDIE MCINTYRE WORKS in the kitchen. When I enter the vast underground chamber, I find him chopping carrots and onions for tonight's shepherd's pie. I walk over and stand beside him at the counter.

"Hello," I say. "I'm Leonard Flint. You're a member of my ward."

"I know, Doc. I met you at supper last night." Bridie doesn't take his eyes from his task. The knife knocks against the chopping board with finality. *No, no, no*, it seems to be saying.

"I just want to know if I can be of any assistance to you," I say. "In any way."

"I'm a little busy now, Doc," says Bridie. "I don't really have time to help you out."

And that's just it, I think, backing out of the kitchen. He would be helping me, not the other way around. The sound of the knife mocks me as I leave—*no, no, no*.

Well, Bridie, I think, *just because you have a concrete task to accomplish doesn't make you a superior being. And Bridie, isn't that a woman's name you have?*

I INHALE THE dark of the stable as though it were the sweetest smoke. I like that I can't see anything right away, and the moments it takes my eyes to adjust to the dimness are like moments of weightlessness, like I am falling backwards through time and I am landing as a boy inside the dark of Sugar Hill.

Bill has one of the horses out of its stall and he's brushing it. When I walk across the floor of the stable towards him, he reaches down and picks up another brush, hands it to me.

"I thought you might be back," he says. "Might as well put you to work."

The horses have been outside much of the morning and their coats are covered in dust. When I sweep the brush in small arcs across the back of the animal, dust rises and hangs in the air, settles on my clothes, finds its way inside my nose and mouth.

"I've been trying to do my job, Bill," I say. "Trying to help the men on my ward. But I don't feel competent enough or old enough. I don't think anyone respects me, or even likes me."

"People are not much good," says Bill. "They never have been. It's no use trying to make them so."

We are standing on opposite sides of the horse. I can feel the great shuddering heat of the animal between us, can see the top of Bill's head above the withers.

"Don't you remember me yet, Bill?"

"Nope."

The horse snorts and stamps its foot and a cloud of dust rises and drifts down the stale air between us.

"I used to come and see you in Sugar Hill. You used to make me bread in your outdoor oven."

"I do recall an oven," says Bill. "Out of doors, as you say." He pauses, leans over the back of the horse, looking at me. "Go on," he says. "Tell me something else to make me remember."

"You had dogs," I say. "Two of them. A grey one and a black one. The grey one was scruffy."

"What were their names?"

"They didn't have names."

Bill grins. "Yes," he says. "That's right. What else? What else do you know about me?"

I put my hand in the pocket of my doctor's coat and take out the rabbits' feet. I've been carrying them around all day. Each time I talked to one of my unco-operative patients, I would put my hand in the pocket of my coat and feel the reassuring softness of the rabbit fur, the hard flex of the bones, the small, sharp nails, and I would feel comforted.

I pass the rabbits' feet over the back of the horse to Bill.

"You gave these to me," I say.

Bill lays the six rabbits' feet beside one another in the palm of his hand. His hand is so big that there's room left over for at least another three rabbits' feet in there.

"These were mine?" he asks.

"They were. You used to sell them in town. In Canwood."

Bill looks at them carefully.

"I must have trapped them first," he says.

"You did."

"What kind of a trap did I use?"

"A snare."

I can see Bill inside his dug-out home in Sugar Hill, holding up the hoop of wire and grinning, then lowering it around my wrist and slowly tightening it to demonstrate how he killed the rabbits.

Bill studies my face. "If I gave you this many feet," he says, "then I must know you. I must have liked you. Do you look very different?"

"I was a boy then."

"A boy, yes," Bill says slowly. "A boy was often kind to me when I lived in Sugar Hill." He tries to pass the rabbits' feet back to me, but I shake my head.

"No," I say. "Let's share them between us. Let's take three each." I reach across and take half of the rabbits' feet and drop them back into my coat pocket. Bill curls his hand around the remaining three.

"All right," he says.

I feel that we have made a promise to each other by doing this; that here in the dark of the stable with the horse standing witness between us, we have agreed to the one thing I have always known to be true: Bill and I belong to each other. We belong together.

LATER THAT NIGHT, in the quiet of my cottage, I try to write up my notes from the day. It is hard to know what to say about each of my encounters with my patients. Each time, I felt, or was made to feel, foolish by my conversations with the men.

I try to say something about Tom Bright. He seems

the easiest to write about. My pen scratches across the page. It's dusk, and when I look up I can see the flight of the swallows over the river. I look down at what I've written.

He seems gentler now, more thoughtful perhaps. He seems strong and kind and tolerant of my attempts at friendship.

I'm not writing of Tom Bright at all. I'm writing about Rabbit Foot Bill.

THE NEXT DAY Dr. Christiansen summons me to attend an LSD session with one of my patients, an alcoholic named Gus Polder. I meet the patient and doctor in Dr. Christiansen's office at ten thirty in the morning.

"Gus has already taken the drug," Dr. Christiansen informs me when I arrive at his office. "We will now ensure that he is relaxed and comfortable while we wait for the LSD to take effect."

Gus Polder is a man in his forties, with the thin build and weather-beaten face of someone who works outside. He perches on the edge of Dr. Christiansen's sofa, his left foot tapping lightly, nervously, against the floor.

"Hiya, Doc," he says.

"Hi," I say back. This is the friendliest exchange I've had yet with anyone on my ward. I don't, however, recognize Gus Polder.

"This is Gus's first session," says Dr. Christiansen. He's sitting down behind his massive oak desk that effectively cuts him off at the chest. I'm thinking that when Gus Polder is under the influence of the drug, he might not appreciate seeing a disembodied head talking to him, but I don't know how to bring this up. Even with Luke Christiansen's assurances that we are equal, that we are colleagues, I never feel this to be true. He always seems to be my boss, and I can't talk freely with him because of this.

"What we are trying to do," continues Dr. Christiansen, "is to recreate the DTs for Mr. Polder, so that by experiencing the worst of being an alcoholic, he will be motivated to stop his addiction."

"I ain't had the DTs yet," says Gus Polder. "Been lucky, I guess." He laughs and then stops, but I notice that his foot tapping has increased in intensity. Gus Polder doesn't look to me like a man who's been lucky at all.

"How can we make him have the DTs?" I ask.

"LSD is a mind-altering drug," says Dr. Christiansen. "We will simply alter his mind while he is under the influence."

"We will intentionally force him to have a bad experience?"

"It's not a bad experience we're after," says Dr. Christiansen. "It's a cautionary experience. We will simply take a shortcut to a place Mr. Polder would have arrived at anyway, and by taking a shortcut we will negate the progressive nature of the alcohol addiction."

"After the artificial DTs, he will be able to effectively stop the need for drinking?"

"I would like that," says Gus Polder, but he looks more anxious than convinced.

"There is always a reason why people take to drink," says Dr. Christiansen. "Come on, Dr. Flint, surely you have learnt something in medical school?"

"There's an emotional root cause," I say.

"Exactly," says Dr. Christiansen. "And what we are hoping to achieve in these sessions is to visit that root cause, to discover what is at the bottom of Mr. Polder's addiction to alcohol."

"I've always liked the taste of beer," says Gus Polder helpfully, but we both ignore this remark.

"So we deliberately induce a bad experience and hope that will release some of the negative emotions that are the cause of his alcoholism?"

"Yes." Dr. Christiansen stands up and comes out from behind his desk. "Now, we need to make the patient comfortable so that the experience is as pleasant as possible."

I don't say that it will be impossible to make someone comfortable if you are setting him up to be uncomfortable. I don't say that it seems risky to me to undertake behaviour modification experiments on people who are perhaps a little mentally frail to begin with.

"What's the success rate?" I ask.

"Very promising," says Dr. Christiansen. "But the data is ongoing. Now, Gus," he says, "I want you to lie on your back and I will put a soft towel across your closed eyes."

"What about my shoes?" says Gus. "They'll mark the fabric."

"Remove your shoes. And lie back."

"There are no definitive findings yet?" I ask.

"We're still in the experimental stages," says Dr. Christiansen. "We won't be able to process the data until the experiments are complete. But the preliminary findings are very promising indeed."

Gus Polder has removed his shoes and tucked them under the sofa. He lies back.

"What are the preliminary findings?" I ask.

"Not now, Flint."

Dr. Christiansen leans over and plumps up the pillow behind Gus's head and then lays a folded white towel across his eyes and forehead.

"How are you feeling?" he asks.

"What if I accidentally fall asleep?" says Gus.

"You won't fall asleep."

"But what if I do?"

"I want you to take notes," says Dr. Christiansen to

me. "You'll find a notebook on my desk. Fetch yourself a pen. Note the time and write down that the patient is experiencing anxiety."

I dutifully do as he says.

"Doc, you haven't answered my question," says Gus Polder.

"You won't fall asleep," says Dr. Christiansen. "We will make sure of that, won't we, Dr. Flint?"

"Sure," I say. "I mean, we'll help you," but I must not sound very convincing because Gus Polder suddenly takes the cloth off his forehead and sits bolt upright.

"I don't think I want to be going through with this," he says. "I don't think I'm ready. I ain't never had the DTs. Why would I want to have them now, when I'm not even drinking?"

"It's too late," says Dr. Christiansen, his hand on Gus's shoulder, trying to ease him back down to a supine position on the sofa. "You can't un-take the drug."

"I could sick it up," says Gus.

"It's already in your system. In fact," says Dr. Christiansen, exerting real pressure trying to push Gus Polder back down on the sofa, "I think it's already working. This nervousness you feel is all part of the drug already working in your system."

There's a moment of silence while we all try to come to terms with this fact.

"You have a problem that needs fixing," says Dr.

Christiansen. "The problem was caused by pain, so the cure won't be painless. Do you understand?"

Gus Polder allows himself to be slowly pushed back down to a prone position. "Yes," he says, a man not so much understanding his fate as resigning himself to it.

"Patient emotionally resistant," says Dr. Christiansen over his shoulder to me, and I write that down in the notebook. Then I cross out the word "resistant" and put down the word "reluctant" instead. Gus Polder's apprehensions about the drug seem reasonable to me. "Resistant" seems too harsh a term to explain it.

"Now, Gus," continues Dr. Christiansen, "are you relatively comfortable lying there with the towel over your eyes?"

"Yes."

"Well then, I want you to describe for Dr. Flint and me what you are seeing in your mind's eye. Could you do that for us?"

"I think so."

There's a silence.

"Any time you want to start would be fine," says Dr. Christiansen.

"It's dark," says Gus.

"Perhaps the drug hasn't really taken effect yet," I say. "He seems to be referring to the towel over his eyes."

"Perhaps not." Dr. Christiansen pulls over his desk chair and sits down on it next to the sofa. "Gus, I want you to remember back to when you were a child. Can you do that for me?"

"I think so."

"What do you think about when you remember being a child?"

"We had a dog I liked. His name was Star."

"What else?"

"We lived on a farm. It were Mr. Morgan's farm. My daddy worked for him. We had a little house in the far corner of the wheat field in sight of the main house."

I sit down on the edge of Dr. Christiansen's desk. I'm not sure what I should be writing down in the notebook. I put down the words *dog* and *tenant farmer*, and then I cross out the word *dog*.

"Were your parents good to you, Gus?" asks Dr. Christiansen.

"My mother died," says Gus. "My older sister, Bernice, looked after us when we were babies. We called her Bernie. It was her dog. Star was her dog."

I write the word *dog* back into the notebook and put a line underneath it.

"What happened to the dog?" I ask.

"Daddy shot it. The dog was to keep him away from Bernie, and when he'd had enough of that, he shot it."

"Did your father hurt all of you?" asks Dr. Christiansen. He's leaning forward on his chair. This is clearly what he wants to hear.

"I don't remember," says Gus Polder.

"I think you do," says Dr. Christiansen.

I feel suddenly that I can't breathe. My collar feels too tight around my neck, and I reach up to loosen it only to find that it's already loose. I hold on to the sides of the desk to stop the dizziness that has started sizzling through me.

"Did you write that down?" says Dr. Christiansen. "Flint? What's the matter with you?"

"I feel a little ill, sir. Must be something I ate at breakfast." I put the notebook and pen down on the desk. "I'm sorry, sir, I just need to get some air. I'll be right back."

Outside in the corridor I squat down with my back against the wall. I try to concentrate on breathing, slowly and surely, in and out and back in again, my head resting in the bowl of my hands.

I remember the dark and the smell of earth and the cold and the way my body hurt like it was broken.

But I won't think that. It's not true. Bill would never harm me. It was always nice when I went to Sugar Hill. There were hay bales with furs on them. There was homemade bread. There was the climb up to the top of the hill and the run back down. There were the dogs and the roses in the garden.

The office door opens and Dr. Christiansen comes out into the hallway.

"Are you feeling too ill to continue?" he asks,

"because I think we're at a critical point. I'm starting to induce the DTs, and you might want to see how this is done."

I push the thoughts of the dark and cold inside Sugar Hill back down into the earth and I close the door on them.

"Yes," I say, standing up. "I'm all right now. I can come back in."

As in the birthday game we sometimes played as children, Dr. Christiansen is making Gus Polder handle various objects and substances and telling him that they are other than they are.

He rests Gus's hand in a small bowl of cold, cooked spaghetti.

"These are worms," he says. "They are worms and they are crawling over your body. Can you feel them? They have started up your arms and legs. They will crawl inside your ears and mouth and try to choke you up."

Gus jerks his hand out of the bowl and starts slapping at his arms and legs. "Get them off me," he says. "Please, get them off me."

"I'm sorry," says Dr. Christiansen, calmly. "There are just too many of them. I can't do anything."

In his frenzied slapping, Gus has knocked the towel from his eyes, but having his eyes open doesn't seem to make any difference to his perception that worms are crawling over the length of his body. In fact, with his eyes open, it's as though he sees them all the more clearly.

"Please help me," he says. "I can feel them burrowing under my skin. They're travelling inside me." He's staring at the veins on his forearm that are standing out from his skin, just like they are worms.

"He's upset," I say. "We should stop."

"No," says Dr. Christiansen. "It's working. When he comes up out of this, he will remember the horror of this experience."

"And you think it will really stop him from wanting to drink?"

"Yes, I do." Dr. Christiansen turns to me from his seat next to Gus Polder. "Are you taking good notes? I'm relying on you."

It's dark, I write. *I'm being held down. My face is in the dirt. I can taste the grit and stick of it in my mouth. There are no sounds from outside. The earth muffles noise. It curls around me like a closed fist.*

"Please help me," moans Gus Polder. I look down at what I've written, rip the page out, crumple it up, and jam it into my pocket.

The patient is in distress, I write. *He thinks that worms are slithering up his body and will make their way into his mouth and ears, choking him. He has remembered the violence he suffered at the hands of his father. He has remembered the rape of his sister and a dog that was shot.*

∽

I'M LYING ON the sofa in my cottage with a folded towel across my eyes when there's a knock at the door.

It's William Scott.

"Hi," he says. "I've come to see if you need anything. Luke said you were feeling ill this morning."

"I'm okay." I don't open the screen door to let him in, and he doesn't open it himself to step inside the cottage. "We gave LSD to Gus Polder and made him experience the DTs."

"I know. Luke told me."

I sit up on the sofa.

"Do you ever remember something you're not sure even happened?" I ask.

"Repressed memories?" William sounds instantly interested. He opens the screen door and comes into the cottage.

"I guess so."

Behind William the river is a coppery snake winding through the field grass. The sun is at such an angle to the surface that I can see the dark lines on the riverbed that must be sunken logs, the holes that must be rocks.

"There was a moment," I say, "when I felt that everything was about me, and not about Gus Polder."

"Maybe you were identifying too strongly with the patient?"

"Maybe. I did find it all a bit upsetting."

"He resisted the treatment?"

"He was reluctant." I felt sorry for Gus, but there was some other shift that happened in that room. "But, no, that's not it."

William Scott comes over and sits beside me on the sofa.

"We could explore that if you'd like," he says. "I could analyze you."

"I don't know." What I have seen so far of psychiatric analysis at the Weyburn has left a lot to be desired. "I'll have to think about it."

"Don't think too much about it, or you'll talk yourself out of it."

"That doesn't exactly fill me with confidence."

William grins and stands up. "You know where to find me," he says. "If you decide to go ahead with it."

After he goes I lie back down on the sofa and replace the towel across my eyes. I think of Gus and how he squirmed and shouted, the obvious terror he felt when he was made to relive his past. Perhaps William was right when he said that I was identifying too strongly with the patient? Perhaps my terror was borrowed from Gus? But the more I take myself down this route, the more I know, at the heart of me, that it is a lie.

∾

WHEN THE SUPPER hour comes, I intercept the food cart in the hallway outside one of the dormitories and take a tray of food. Instead of going to eat in the kitchen with my patients, I take the supper tray back outside and head over to the stables.

The August night is coming on. Already there is the faint shape of the moon hammered into the dusky sky. The first star shines bright above the river.

Bill is sitting in his stall, his tray of food balanced on his lap. He moves along the bed so there's room for me to sit down, and I sit down next to him, put my tray of food across my lap in imitation of him. I can feel the shudder down the row of stalls as a horse rubs his coat against the boards.

Bill eats noisily. I can hear the muscles in his jaw popping as he chews. He holds the tray steady with one hand and shovels the food in with the other. He barely pauses for breath.

I run my fork over the potato crust of the shepherd's pie on my tray, and when Bill has finished with his supper, I slide mine along to him.

"You can have it too," I say. "I don't feel much like eating."

Bill grunts in response and dispatches my meal with the same admirable efficiency as he finished his own. When he's done he puts both trays on the floor, one piled neatly on top of the other, and he stands up, wipes his hands on the front of his trousers.

"I've work to do," he says, dismissing me.

"I could help you."

Bill stands beside the bed, staring down at me with a look in his eyes that I can't quite read. He seems to be assessing both whether I can do the work that's required and whether or not he wants my company while doing it.

"You should take your white coat off then," he says after a moment. "It will get dirty."

I help him muck out the stalls and put new straw down for the horses. We work without speaking under the light of the bare bulbs that hang on their cords over the aisle outside the stalls.

I like the weight of the pitchfork and the smell of the clean straw. I like feeling the prickle of sweat starting at the back of my neck. I look at my doctor's coat, folded over the door of a stall. How proud I was when I first put that coat on. How relieved I feel now to have taken it off.

Bill is a strong and steady worker and we just do what we have to do until it's done, moving methodically down the row of stalls until, at the last one, he shovels the horseshit out and sluices down the floor with a pail of water, and I spread the new straw. We refill the water buckets and give the horses each a small nosebag of oats. Then we lead them back into their stalls and latch each of the doors.

The bulbs swing on their cords where the horses have brushed against them when they were ambling back into their berths. The air is close and hot. I wipe my forehead with the sleeve of my white shirt.

"Let's go outside," I say to Bill.

He follows me through the stable door. The night feels as cool as water on my skin. There are the sounds of crickets and the low loop of an owl across the fields.

"Let's lie down on the grass," I say, and we stretch out on our backs, an arm's length apart.

"Bill," I say, "what happened to you after you were taken away from Canwood?"

"That was a long time ago," says Bill. "I don't like to think on it."

"But do you remember?"

"Some of it." Bill sighs. It's a sound like the horses make. "Most of it," he says.

"What happened first? What happened when they took you out of the courtroom after the verdict?"

"They put me in a truck," Bill says. "With no windows. The truck went fast. All fast and bumpy. I didn't know where I was. It was just a box with no windows in the back of the truck."

"They took you to the prison?"

"They put me down a hole," says Bill, "and fed me through a slot in the door."

"Did they hurt you?"

"Not right away."

"Did they work you?"

"I wouldn't have minded that," says Bill. "But mostly I was kept in the hole. I could put my arms out and touch the walls. It were like a grave."

I remember an article from medical school that described the rationale behind the building of the early prisons. The cells *were* meant to resemble graves. It psychologically unhinges a man if he can touch the walls of his cell with arms outstretched. This was meant to be part of the punishment, this psychological unhinging. They wanted the prisoners to become insane from their isolation and confinement.

"What did you think about?" I ask. "When you were in your cell?"

"Nothing."

"Nothing at all?"

Bill sighs. "There was no point," he says, "in thinking of anything, because I couldn't change where I was. Even in my thoughts. I couldn't get out of that hole in the ground."

There seems like no worse hell to me. I hate to think of Bill's suffering during those years.

"You must have been glad when they moved you," I say.

"Yes."

"It's a very different place here."

"I like it," says Bill. "I like the horses, and the people leave me alone." He pauses. "Except for you," he says.

"Do you mind? Do you mind that I come to see you?"

Bill is quiet for a moment. "No," he says softly, and I can tell from the nearness of his voice that he's turned his head towards me, that he's watching me. "I might even like it, Dr. Lenny."

We lie on our backs under the rattle of stars. We push our breath out in unison, haul it in again, until our breathing makes engines of our bodies in the dark.

THE MOTHS KNOCK against the porch light and the moon is climbing the sky above the river when I get back to my cottage. My body is stiff from lying so long in the grass outside the stables with Bill. I realize too that I left my white lab coat in the stables, folded over the door of one of the stalls. It's too late to go back for it now. I'll have to remember to get it first thing in the morning. I feel a twinge of guilt for shirking my responsibilities at the Weyburn. I had wanted to do so well at this job, but now I can't seem to concentrate on it at all.

But really, I'm not that bothered by forgetting the coat, or by the stiffness in my limbs, or by my dereliction of duty. I feel happy at having spent the evening hours with Bill. While he still might not remember exactly who I am, he is at least opening up to me, and it feels like we are finally connecting.

I lie on my bed, fully clothed, with the lights out, and

I think of lying on the grass beside Bill. It is the first time since I got to the Weyburn that I haven't felt slightly out of control, that I haven't been rushing. It is the first time that I've felt completely in my own skin. Why would I feel like that if something bad had happened to me as a child at Sugar Hill? The memories that I had while I was witnessing Gus Polder's LSD journey make no sense to me when I lie them alongside that moment at the stables with Bill, when I felt so peaceful and happy.

The next morning I rush into the stables on my way to breakfast. Bill and the horses are gone, out working in the fields presumably, but my coat is right where I left it the night before, neatly folded over the stall door. I take it down and put it on and walk back outside again. I am disappointed not to have seen Bill. I had been thinking about nothing else on my walk over to the stables. Our conversation of the night before has made me hungry for further contact.

I head towards the hospital, and then I change my mind and turn around, walk back down the path towards the farm fields. I don't need to speak to him. I just want sight of him. Seeing him will be enough to assuage my disappointment in not finding him in the stables when I went to get my coat. Seeing him will be enough of a fix for me to get through this day.

The horses are pulling a thresher. I can spot them in the distance, can see the hay falling beneath the blades of the machine. And if I get up on the fence, stand on the lower rung and balance myself against the upper rung, I can see the small figure of Bill out in front of the horses, leading them forward through the August morning.

DR. CHRISTIANSEN STOPS me in the corridor on my way to the ward kitchen.

"How are you managing, Flint?" he asks.

"Fine, sir."

He puts a hand on my shoulder.

"You've recovered from the incident the other morning?"

"Yes, sir." I have completely forgotten about my reaction to Gus Polder's LSD experiment. "It must have been something I ate, sir."

Dr. Christiansen keeps his hand on my shoulder and squeezes it gently.

"I've let you have your head," he says. "But I think it's been long enough for that. You've had enough time to get settled in properly by now. I need to have a look at what you are doing."

"You do?"

"I'll trail you during your rounds. Say, next Thursday morning. We can start out here, Flint." He takes his hand away from my shoulder. "Nine o'clock. Sharp."

For Dr. Christiansen to accompany me on my rounds,

I need to have rounds. I have less than a week to invent a routine that seems like it's been in place from the day I arrived at the mental hospital.

After breakfast I walk over to the mattress factory. When Henry Tudor sees me coming, he scuttles to the back of the room. But I know better this time. I approach the supervisor first. He's in a small office by the bolts of ticking, typing clumsily on a portable typewriter.

"Hiya, Doc," he says. "You're back." He pulls the sheet of paper from the typewriter and lays it on the desk. "Order forms," he says. "They'll be the death of me. We seem to run out of something every second day." He puts both hands behind his head and leans back in his chair. "What can I do for you, Doc?" he says. "Are you here to have another dance with Two Step?"

"No, I think I'll sit this one out." I move a few feet farther into the room. "I want to know who's ready for a job outside of this hospital. Who are your best workers?"

"Well," says the supervisor, "my best workers aren't necessarily the ones who are fit for the outside world. Two Step is actually quite a good worker, but it wouldn't do to set him loose in town."

"One man," I say. "Just tell me the name of one man who is ready for outside employment."

"Rusty Kirk," says the supervisor. "You'll find him third sewing machine from the wall on the left-hand side."

Rusty Kirk is a man in his late thirties with an impressive mop of curly red hair. I can see the shine of his hair from across the room.

"Mr. Kirk?"

He looks up from his sewing machine. His mouth is a little twisted and there's a long scar running down his cheek. "I'm Rusty Kirk," he says.

"I'm Leonard Flint. Dr. Leonard Flint. You're on my ward."

"Did I do something, Doc?"

I feel like I'm incompetent in my job, but my patients always assume they're guilty of something, that they've transgressed. The power lies with me, even though it often feels otherwise. I would do well to remember this.

"No, of course not. It just seems time to help you make the transition from this hospital job to a job in town."

The procedure for work placement is for the patient to take an outside job and continue to sleep at the hospital until he's adjusted well enough to his new circumstances to live away from the hospital environment. It's acclimatization by degrees.

"What sort of a job would you like to have?" I ask.

Rusty Kirk looks around the room. "I'd probably be all right at cutting cloth," he says.

"No, not here. If you could have any job, a job not in the hospital, what would that be?"

Rusty knits his brow together in a thoughtful scowl. "I wouldn't mind being a race car driver," he says.

"You like cars then?"

"Yes."

"What about working as a mechanic's helper?"

Rusty looks up at me as though I'm an idiot. "That's not being a race car driver," he says. "That's not driving a race car."

"You have to start somewhere," I say. "You can't start by being a race car driver."

"But you asked me what job I wanted?"

"Well, I said it the wrong way round. The question now is would you like to work with cars?"

"I suppose so," says Rusty grudgingly. "But that wasn't the question a moment ago."

My exchange with Rusty Kirk is turning out like all my other exchanges with the patients at the Weyburn, but I refuse to be defeated this time. There's too much at stake for me to back down.

"All right then," I say. "I'll make some inquiries and I'll be by later to let you know what I've found out." I turn and walk away from Rusty before he is able to protest again about it not being possible for him to be a race car driver.

I spend the morning making phone calls, and after lunch I go back into the mattress factory to collect Rusty Kirk.

"I've lined up an interview for you," I say. "At Scully's Garage. We'll go over there now and I'll bring you back in time for supper."

Rusty Kirk rather reluctantly gets up from his sewing machine and follows me out of the shop. I can feel someone watching us, and when I turn at the door, I see Henry Tudor staring after me.

We take a taxi to Scully's Garage. Tom Scully meets us outside and we all shake hands by the pyramid of oil cans stacked between the gas pumps.

"I've had the mentals before," Scully says to me. "They're good workers."

"Boy," he says to Rusty, even though they're about the same age, "do you think you could pump gas and check oil?"

"Sure."

"And sweep the garage floor, and put the tools back where they came from at the end of the day?" Tom Scully leads us into the mechanics' bays and shows us a pegboard wall where the tools are hung. In the spaces where the tools are missing, there are drawn outlines of wrenches or saws or hammers that used to occupy those spots.

"That's clever," says Rusty.

"You could do that?" asks Tom Scully.

"Sure." Rusty seems more childlike, more defenceless and obedient, out of the hospital setting.

"Job's yours then," says Tom Scully to Rusty. To me he says, "I'll have to pay him a little less for the favour I'm doing you."

Before I call for the taxi to drive us back to the hospital, I take Rusty Kirk for a coffee and a piece of pie at the restaurant across the road from Scully's Garage.

"Do you think you'll be all right there?" I ask Rusty as we're standing at the pastry case, choosing our pies.

"Mr. Scully seems like a nice man."

"Nice enough, I suppose." He doesn't seem nice to me at all. He seems a man who's on to a good scheme and knows it. "But if he gives you any trouble, any trouble at all, you're to tell me about it. Understand?"

"Do you think I could have the lemon meringue?" says Rusty. "I like how high it is."

We sit at the counter on the red vinyl stools that turn right around, and eat our pie and drink our coffee.

"Why are you in the Weyburn?" I ask.

"There were too many of us. Someone had to go." Rusty takes an enormous forkful of pie. "Daddy said I wasn't right in the head and I should go into the bughouse. Be one of the bugs in the bughouse." He shovels the pie into his mouth and tries to say something else with his mouth full of meringue.

"What?"

"Boys eat too much. That's what Daddy said."

"How long have you been inside?"

"Since I was eight."

Probably there was not much wrong with Rusty Kirk before he was put into the mental hospital. Thirty-odd years of living as a mental defective have transformed him into one. Now he'll pump gas and sweep out the greasy floors of the mechanics' bays for the rest of his life. Now he'll be cheap labour for a man like Tom Scully. The injustice of this rises in me like bile, leaving a sour taste at the back of my throat.

"Would you like another piece of pie?" I ask.

Rusty, with his mouth full of the first piece, nods, and I wave the waitress over to get him another slice.

BILL IS WAITING supper for me. When I burst into the stables at the end of the day, having lost half my food on the rush over, he's sitting on the edge of his bed, his untouched tray balanced on his lap.

"You don't have to wait for me," I say, dropping down beside him. "I might not always be able to come. I might get stuck on the ward."

But as I say this, I think, *I will always try to be here. I will always try to find you.*

Bill doesn't say anything in reply. He just waits until I pick up my fork, and then he picks up his and we begin eating. Supper is meatloaf and gravy, potatoes, carrots, peas. The dessert is a rather lardy peach pie, not nearly

as good as the piece of pie I had earlier at the restaurant
in town with Rusty Kirk.

When we're finished eating, Bill takes my tray and
puts it on the floor next to his. Then he reaches over
and slides the white coat from my shoulders, removing
it and folding it neatly and placing it on the upturned
wooden box that functions as a small table by his bed.

"Do you want me to help you muck out the horses?"
I ask.

Bill shakes his head.

"Do you not like the white coat?"

"No. It makes you look like a doctor."

"But I am a doctor."

Perhaps, to relate to me, Bill has to separate me from
my profession, from the bad associations with doctors
that he might have experienced at the Weyburn before
I got here.

"All right," I say. "I don't have to be a doctor here."
I certainly don't feel like one when I'm out with Bill in
the stables.

He sits back down beside me on the cot. "That's better," he says.

"Bill," I say, "what were you like when you were a
boy?"

I remember people in the little town where we
both used to live saying that Bill had come from farther
north, that he'd worked his way down the rail line and

had ended up in Canwood only a few years before my family moved there.

Bill is quiet for a moment and I think he hasn't heard me.

"What was your childhood like?" I ask. "Where did you live? What did your father do?"

Bill shrugs.

"You don't remember?" I ask.

"I don't care," he says.

From my training, I know that a closed door means a walk around the house to find the open window.

"When I was a boy," I say, "I had you. Who did you have?"

"No one."

"There must have been someone?"

Bill is quiet for a moment. "I had a dog," he says.

"What was his name?"

"Didn't have one." Bill looks square at me. "He was a dog," he says. "What good would a name do?"

I remember the trial, and my blind rush out to Sugar Hill. I remember the open door to Bill's house, and the trampled garden, how I ran up to the top of the hill, but the dogs were nowhere in sight.

"I went to look for your dogs, just like you asked me to at the trial. But I couldn't find them. They'd been eating the rabbits for a while, but then they must have left."

"A dog will go," says Bill, "when the food goes. Then there's no point in staying."

"Is that what happened to your dog? When you were a boy? Did it just go?"

Bill rubs his face with his hands. "I don't remember," he says.

"Did it die?"

"I don't know."

"I'm sorry you don't remember," I say.

Bill leans over and pats me on the knee. "It's all right," he says. "You looked for them."

He thinks I'm still talking about his dogs on Sugar Hill. I don't correct him.

The stable murmurs with animal noise and the creak and shift of the wooden boards of the building. It is like a skin that holds us all within it, that covers the whisper of our blood, the snap of our bones.

"I'm not doing well here," I say to Bill.

"I know," he says, and this surprises me.

"How do you know?"

"You don't settle. When something's frightened, it doesn't settle. I see you rushing about, afraid to land."

I suddenly feel exhausted.

"Am I frightened?" I ask. "I'm tired, and I don't know why. There's no good reason for it."

Perhaps if I had tried harder to do my job and learn the place, instead of each day still seeming like it's my first day. I feel I'm losing competence rather than gaining it.

Bill stands up, and I move to follow him.

"No," he says, and he pushes me back down on the bed, firmly but gently. "You rest here. I'll watch out for you."

I lie back down on the scratchy blanket, on the lumpy mattress probably stuffed by Henry Tudor, and I promptly fall asleep.

When I wake, all the lights in the stable are out. I can see the glint of the moon through the boards high up near the rafters, can hear the heavy shuffle of the horses, and something else, something closer. There's a snoring noise nearby. I raise myself up on an elbow and look over the edge of the bed and see Bill, curled up on the hard floor like a dog, beside my cot.

THERE'S ALWAYS A place outside of a story from where that story is told. It can't be told from the inside. How can it be? The story must be over before it can be told. There must be a beginning and a middle and an end, and the person telling the story must know them all. From the beginning, if you are telling the story, you must be able to see the end, just as though you were standing at the top of a tall hill, looking out into the distance.

But sometimes there are moments inside a story that could operate as the ending, which feel like an ending. And the moment when Bill let me sleep, when he said those words, "I'll watch out for you," that felt like an ending, the right ending for me. If the story had only stopped there, then everything would have turned out all right. That would have been the happy ending.

I LOOK OVER the edge of the bed, at Bill curled up on the floor, and I think of something I came across when I was in medical school. It was a photograph, presented as scientific curiosity, but I believed in it, in the idea behind the taking of the photograph.

In the summer of 1892 August Strindberg, playwright and artist, tried to photograph the human soul. The soul he tried to photograph was his own, with a series of blurry black and white portraits. In the one I saw, he stares out at the camera, his eyes dark and defiant, his overcoat undone. He is standing in front of a wooden door and his head is in the centre of the photograph—the door rises like a sail behind him—as though the weight of this act, the baring of his soul, has sunk him down inside the frame.

I think we were meant to regard the photograph as a delightful folly, a spiritual aside, but I believed it was true. I think that there are moments when the human soul is visible, and what I was seeing when I looked over the side of the bed at Bill curled up on the floor, was a glimpse of his soul. And what is a soul? Something between the inherent nature of an individual, and their desires—a tangible truth and a reaching, all bound up together. Like the movement of the rabbit in flight, how it runs so fast that its feet don't touch the ground.

I lie back down on the scratchy blanket, but I can't fall asleep again. Instead I listen to the rasp of Bill's breathing and the sound of the horses in their stalls. I can feel my own heart beating in my throat, like a word murmured over and over, like a name—*Bill, Bill, Bill*—swimming through my body.

It's LATE WHEN I get back to my cottage, but Agatha is waiting for me, sitting on the porch steps, smoking. Her cigarette flickers like a firefly in the summer darkness. I can see it before I can see her.

"Well, hello," she says when I walk towards her across the grass. "I was just about to give up."

"I was working late," I say. My heart has given a little leap at seeing her sitting there. "And I wasn't expecting you."

"Well, you can never expect me," she says. "But isn't that what keeps it exciting?"

"I suppose."

"Luke has gone out of town for the night. He has a meeting in Regina with the hospital board first thing in the morning, and he likes to already be there the day of the meeting, rather than to be driving towards it. It helps with his clarity of mind. That's his reasoning. Or what he tells me. But maybe he has a secret girlfriend that I don't know about."

I open the door and we go into the cottage.

"Do you really think so?" I ask.

"It would be easier if he did, wouldn't it?" she says.

"Less guilt."

"Much less guilt." She kisses me. And then it doesn't matter if Luke Christiansen has a girlfriend. What matters is that he has left for Regina and won't be back until the next day.

"You can stay all night then?" I say.

"What's left of it. I've been here ages already. Waiting for you."

We undress slowly, make love with the windows open so that we can hear the crickets and the call of the owl. Afterwards, we lie on our backs in the dark, our bodies still slick with sweat and come, holding hands.

"We could go for a swim," I say. "The river would feel pretty nice right about now."

"Too risky. Someone might see us. Besides, I don't really like swimming."

"How could anyone not like swimming?"

"In England, swimming is done in the sea, and the sea is always cold and wavy."

I roll over on my side so I can look at her.

"What was it like where you lived in England?"

"We were in a small village," says Agatha. "It was quite posh and snobby. People were very concerned with their roses and the amount of horseshit on the bridle path."

"Is that all?" I think of the multitude of things I could say about where I come from, about Canwood, how I could talk for at least an hour on the look of the prairie grass swaying in the fields, or the approach of a storm, or the sound the poplar leaves made in the wind.

"Of course not." Agatha rolls onto her side as well, strokes my face with her hand. "But it would make me sad to talk about my life there, and I don't want to feel sad right now."

We kiss. She trolls her fingers across my shoulders, down my back.

"Oh," she says, suddenly pulling away from me. "That's a shame." Her voice is low and tender.

"What?"

She still has her hand on my back, is feeling around between my shoulder blades. "You have welts. Scars."

"That's nothing," I say. "I played outside as a child. There were a lot of brambles. Once, I got caught in some barbed wire near the depot." My skin was always scratched and torn. There were always stitches of blood laced across my body.

"That's good." Agatha sounds relieved. "Because I don't like to think of you being hurt."

This makes me smile. "Then you might care about me, just a little?"

"I might. Just a little." She kisses me again, harder, and the sound of night outside the window dissolves into our ragged breathing, the quick skitter of my heart in my chest.

WILLIAM SCOTT ACCOMPANIES me to the hospital the next morning. Agatha disappeared before sunrise, leaving me to wake and wonder if it had all been a dream, then shower and dress, walk outside to find William just leaving his cottage. I hope that he hasn't heard Agatha and me having sex, but there is nothing in his manner to suggest that he has, no change that I can gauge in how he interacts with me.

"Beautiful morning," he says, beaming at me. He always seems to be cheerful and I want to ask him how he manages this, but I don't know him well enough for that sort of question.

We walk across the grass. The dew glints and sparkles in the sunlight.

"Have you thought anymore about your repressed memories?" asks William.

"I had forgotten about them," I say, and we both laugh.

"Well, I haven't," he says. "In fact I've given them quite a lot of pondering. We could always take LSD together, you know. I could lead you through a session, take notes. That might unstick things for you."

I remember Gus Polder and how much of his experience under LSD seemed unpleasant. But I have seen him on the ward since then, and he does seem improved somehow—lighter, not so careworn.

"Maybe," I say.

"We could do it in your cottage," says William. "No need to have it take place in the hospital. It could be completely private. Just between us. I really think that it might help. Here." He hands me a booklet. "Have a look at this when you get the chance." It's the handbook on LSD that we give our patients, to let them know what to expect when they are under the influence of the drug. I have never actually read it all, and certainly not from the perspective of becoming a patient myself.

I open it up when I get to my office and look at the questionnaire that the drug-taker is supposed to fill out after the experience. The questions range from the positive—*Did you feel that you could share other people's feelings? Did you feel that you were able to think on different levels? Did you feel in the experience like laughing at many of the ideas you held prior to it? Did you feel a close spiritual bond or unity with others?*—to the negative—*Did you find yourself too weak to move about much of the time? Did you fear that you might die during the experience? Did you feel that you were insane at any time?*—to the simply baffling—*Did you feel that other people were influencing your thoughts against your will? Did you feel at times that you were more than one person?*

According to the handbook the most intense part of the experience is the first two hours. That isn't very long, but even so, I'm not sure I can go through two hours of not feeling in control, of feeling like I might die or that I was more than one person.

At lunchtime I go out to the stables, looking for Bill. I know as soon as I enter the building that he isn't there. I can sense it. It's almost as though I can smell it, can smell his absence. He must be out in the fields, exercising or working the horses. There's only one horse still in his stall. He snickers as I walk past and I reach out and touch his soft, wet nose.

It is always the same in Bill's small room, and I like that. There is the neatly made bed and the wooden box table beside it with a flashlight and a glass of water. Bill's clean clothes are folded and placed in a corner of the stall. I look around for the rabbits' feet but don't see them out anywhere. It pleases me to think that Bill might carry them on his body, tucked into the pocket of his overalls, that he might put his hand in that pocket during his working day and feel the soft rabbit fur, the sharp needles of the toenails.

I lie down on the bed, face down so I can inhale the scent of him. It's almost animal, his smell, sharp and strong, a mix of sweat and earth and hay, with a sweet, heavy undertone of rotting fruit.

I think of William Scott's offer to lead me through an LSD experience. It might help explain my compulsion towards Bill. But then I think of the smell of earth and dark, and the way my heart blooms in my throat whenever I see Bill. The sad truth is that I don't think I want to know what's beneath our friendship. I don't know that I want to be cured.

At dinnertime I am at the stables again. Bill is waiting for me, his tray of food balanced on his knees, untouched. He looks up when I enter his stall. I sit down beside him on the bed.

"Where's your food?" says Bill.

"I was late. Trying to catch up on some paperwork. I didn't have time to go and get my supper."

Bill pushes his tray across to me. "You can have mine," he says.

I push it back. "No, I can't," I say. "I'm fine. I can fetch myself something later. You need to eat. You've been working hard all day outside. I haven't. I've just been sitting at a desk."

Bill seems unconvinced. "I could cut my meat in half," he says.

"No, really." I put my hand on top of his to stop him doing this. His skin feels as rough as tree bark. "You don't need to."

Bill saws at his meat. It's pot roast tonight, and mashed potatoes, and green beans. He jams some of the meat and potatoes onto his fork and leans across to me.

"Open your mouth," he says.

I do as he says.

I can't explain, even now, the relief I felt in those moments with Bill, when he ordered me to do something and I just complied. What I depended on with Bill was that there were no social niceties. He said and did only what he wanted to say and do. Relating to him was on an animal level. It was a question of wills and willingness. If his need to do something was greater than my need not to have it done, then I would relent. If my need to resist was greater than his need to insist, then I would stand firm. Dealing with him I always knew how I felt, something that was often absent for me when dealing with anyone else.

He feeds me supper the way birds feed their young, and I accept each forkful of food with gratitude. When we're finished he puts the tray on the floor and offers me a drink from the glass of water by the bed.

"Thank you," I say, but there's really no need to offer

him those words. Bill did not give me half his supper for my thanks. He did it because he decided it needed to be done.

I think again of William Scott's offer. I don't necessarily want to talk about Bill, but there is something I want to talk to Bill about.

"Bill," I say, "I need to know about the murder."

Bill sighs. "I don't like to think on it," he says.

"But I don't understand," I say, "why you would kill that boy. You're not a killer."

"I don't like to think on it."

"But why did you do it?"

Bill gets up and begins to pace the stall, turning quickly when he reaches an end wall and then starting back again.

"Why did you do it, Bill?"

Maybe, the way William has offered to help me, I could help Bill get to the bottom of why he killed Sam Munroe? Maybe I should lead him through an LSD experience?

Bill walks past the bed and accidentally kicks the supper tray, scattering the utensils and bits of food across the floor of the stall. He drops immediately to the ground and starts picking things up, putting them back on the tray.

"Can't make a mess," he says. "I can't make a mess, can't make a mess. There mustn't be a mess."

"It's okay." I get down on the floor to help him pick up the remnants of supper. "I'll help you clean this up. There won't be a mess. It's okay. You won't get into trouble."

And while he hasn't spoken about the penitentiary, except to describe the cell he was kept in, I can tell from Bill's behaviour that he was punished there. He was never a fearful man, so the punishments must have been severe, and the misdeeds small.

WILLIAM SCOTT AND I swim in the river at sunset, the colours of the sky showing on the surface of the water as pink and orange.

"Have you done LSD with a patient yet?" I ask as we breaststroke up to the willow tree and turn for the home stretch.

"Yes. Just once."

"What was it like?"

"Well, Luke had told me before we started that it would be like the two of us were on the same journey, and that I shouldn't try to control the experience. And it was much like that."

"What happened?"

William flips over on his back and floats there. I put my feet down. The water comes to just below my neck. I can feel the slippery skin of a sunken log under my outstretched feet.

"I tried to remember what Luke had said, and just let go of expectations. For a while it worked. I was able to concentrate on the patient, and it was like our minds were floating free and able to meet each other on another plane. But then . . ." William looks over at me. "Then I started to notice the dirt under the patient's fingernails. He had very long fingernails and I couldn't stop looking at them. I could see the dirt as individual pieces but no longer dirt-sized. More like enormous boulders. By then I wasn't paying attention to what he was saying, and his words just seemed to be bubbling over my head. I couldn't understand anything. It was like being underwater."

William grins at me.

"I don't think it could be classified as a success, even from an experimental standpoint."

I think of how upset Bill became at the slightest thing, the spilling of his dinner tray. His reaction to his small act of clumsiness was extreme enough that I know he would never tolerate the vicissitudes of an LSD experience, and that leading him through such an experience would be no help to him at all.

"Would you do it again?" I ask William.

I expect him to say no and am surprised when he has the opposite assessment.

"Yes," he says. "I didn't say it wasn't interesting. I just didn't think it was very helpful."

I MAKE AGATHA a picnic on my bed after we have made love. Cheese and crackers, a cut-up peach, a bottle of wine, a bar of good chocolate.

"Fancy," she says, reading the label on the Camembert.

"I went all the way to Regina to get it," I say. "I had to take the bus and then walk several blocks."

This is the sort of comment that would have driven Amy mad, but Agatha just kisses me on the shoulder.

"You're sweet," she says.

I think of Amy again and how she would have said that to me as an insult. "Isn't that a weak thing?"

"Not in my books." Agatha runs her hand over my shoulder blades. "Make sure you don't change that, even if someone hurts you."

It seems a strange thing to say.

"You're not planning on hurting me, are you?" I ask.

Agatha kisses me to shut me up. Her mouth is sweet from the peach she has just eaten.

Before she leaves she tells me about the party that Dr. Christiansen is throwing the next evening at their house.

"You need to make sure you come," she says.

"But I haven't even been invited?" No one has said anything to me about a party.

"You will be. Luke likes to leave it to the last minute

so there is no chance of backing out. He will also frame it as a team-building exercise so that you will feel obligated to show up."

"Is it?"

"Is it what?"

"Team-building."

Agatha snorts. "It's a drunken catastrophe, that's what it is," she says. "But you need to be there, because by your absence you will be conspicuous. And I can't have him suspecting anything."

"But won't it be awkward?"

"No." Agatha pokes me gently in the chest. "Because you and I will behave impeccably. No longing looks or furtive touching."

"Nothing?"

"Nothing at all."

BUT IT ISN'T nothing to be inside the house where Agatha Christiansen lives. It isn't nothing to see her coats lined up neatly in the hall closet when I go to hang up my jacket. It isn't nothing to see the vase of flowers on the hall table and to think that she picked those blossoms herself this morning. Nor is it nothing to see the photo of her children on the living room mantelpiece, two boys of staggered heights stiffly standing in their school uniforms in front of a brick wall covered in ivy.

"Flint!" yells Luke Christiansen, from across the room.

I wade through the furniture towards him. There are doctors and nurses on all the chairs, and on the two sofas near the fireplace. There are even people perched on the coffee table between the sofas. Everyone is smoking and drinking. The air is a fog of smoke and I can hear the musical notes of the ice shifting in the glasses as I clamber over legs and feet on my way to Dr. Christiansen.

"Good to see you!" He slaps me on the back.

"Yes, sir. You too."

"You made it!"

I know that he means that I have made it to the party, but I also take it to mean that I have successfully completed the difficult journey across the bodies in the living room to get to him.

"I did, sir."

"Fetch yourself a drink, Flint. There's a bar in the kitchen. Agatha will see to you."

I make the return journey over the limbs of the doctors and nurses.

Agatha is by herself in the kitchen, standing by the sink and loading little glass dishes of cocktail sausages and olives onto a silver tray.

"You're meant to see to me," I say. "Orders from your husband."

"Is that so?" She grins. "Would you like me to pour you a drink then, Dr. Flint?"

"No, thank you. I don't really like drinking. I'm not much good at it." I think of the handful of drunken parties I attended in medical school, every one of which ended up with me hanging over a toilet bowl being violently ill later in the evening.

I look back through the open door into the living room. Dr. Hepner is moving around on all fours on the carpet and there is a nurse astride his back, hitting his behind with a rolled-up magazine.

"They all seem to have been here ages ahead of me," I say.

"They just got right down to business," says Agatha. "No time was wasted in pleasantries."

"I don't know that I can go back out there," I say.

"Here." Agatha passes me the tray of hors d'oeuvres. "You can hide behind this."

We work together. She loads the tray with food and I weave through the bodies in the living room, delivering the devilled eggs, sausages, olives on toothpicks, cream cheese pinwheel sandwiches. When the tray is empty, I clutch it to my chest like a battleground shield and head back to the kitchen so that Agatha can fill it up again.

As she asked, and as I promised, we do not kiss or touch, but it feels good to be around her nonetheless, and maybe, if anyone was watching, they would notice the easy way she leans towards me when handing me the stack of paper napkins, or the way my body slouches in her direction when I balance against the counter, waiting for the tray to be refilled.

"As soon as they're drunk enough," she says, when we're standing by the stove, waiting for the sausage rolls to heat up, "you can flee this sinking ship."

"I wish you could too."

She gives me a strange look.

"I live here."

"But you don't belong here."

"Maybe not." Agatha opens the oven door. "But it's where I have to be."

When there are as many party guests passed out as standing, I make my escape, grabbing my jacket from the hall closet, not even bothering to put it on, but sprinting out into the night, the quiet darkness a balm after the mayhem inside the Christiansen home. It's more than a few miles back to my cottage, but I am not worried about that. I could have called for a taxi, but I welcome the long walk. It will help to clear my head.

I start down the drive, and when I'm past the line of parked cars, I turn and look back at the house and see Agatha framed in the lighted kitchen window. I wave and she blows me a kiss.

THE NEXT DAY is Wednesday. Dr. Christiansen is to come with me on my rounds on Thursday. I need to be seen to be doing my job. I need another recruit. But the problem with life at Weyburn is that, for some, it is just too familiar and comfortable a place and there is not a lot of interest shown by the patients in making a change to the unfamiliar outside world.

I try the kitchen again, but there are no takers. I corner a man mopping the ward hallways, practically forcing him out a window in my eagerness to enlist him in my scheme, but he wriggles out from under my arm and runs off, leaving his mop and bucket and a length of dirty hall.

It is no use. The only way I am going to get the patients to agree to what I want is to get to know them. I decide to have dinner on the ward tonight. There isn't time to let Bill know that I won't be able to make it out to the stables to join him, but I figure that he will work out that I'm not able to come when I simply don't show up.

Everyone is quiet when I take a seat at the table in the ward kitchen. It is not like the last time I was here, when each man petitioned me with personal requests. Has it been that long since the last time? Do they regard me suspiciously now because I haven't dealt with their problems and don't even know their names?

"Please pass the potatoes," I say to the man next to me, and he shoves the bowl along the table.

"Could you pour me a glass of water?" I ask another patient, and he upends the water pitcher into my glass so that some of the water sloshes out and runs over the edge of the table onto my foot.

So they are upset with me. I don't mean anything to them, and I don't know how to mean something to them. I look out at the impassive faces of these strangers and I can't see how I will ever be able to change their minds about me, how I will ever be able to do the job that I was hired to do.

After dinner is over I go out to the stables to apologize to Bill for not dining with him tonight.

When I walk into his stall, I find him sitting on the edge of his bunk with his dinner tray on his lap, the food uneaten.

"What's the matter?" I ask. "Why haven't you had your supper?"

Bill looks up at me, his face tired and pale.

"I was waiting for you," he says. "I didn't want to start without you."

I'M IN MY office early the next morning, going through the notebook where I had my patients write down their requests. It had occurred to me in the night that I could perhaps turn this into something I had already done, not something that I was ignoring and would perhaps never do. What if I pretended to Dr. Christiansen that these petitions from the men had already been dealt with? What if this list of complaints was actually a list of successes? I start writing the items down on a separate piece of paper, under the heading *Results*.

I don't notice Agatha standing in my office doorway until she clears her throat and I look up at the sound. It is a surprise to see her there. I jerk upright when she enters the room and bang my knees on the underside of the desk.

"Hi," I say.

Agatha has never once come to my office before. All of our meetings take place at my cottage, aside from our chaste time serving food at the party the other night.

"Hi, yourself."

She stands in the doorway, not moving, just looking at me. I can't read her eyes, but she looks sadder than usual, and maybe also more loving.

"What is it?"

She sighs and steps into my office, closing the door gently behind her.

"This feels worse than I thought it would."

"What does?"

"I have to tell you something," Agatha says. "And it's not something that will make you happy."

The shiver I feel through my body when she says those words tells me that I have deeper feelings for Agatha than I had suspected.

"Please. You said you wouldn't hurt me."

"Well, no, I didn't. If you remember correctly, I didn't say anything. You asked, but I didn't answer."

I know she is right. I remember the taste of peach on her tongue, so sweet and soft.

"So you do intend to hurt me?" I ask.

"This is so much harder than I thought it would be," she says. She advances into the room. "I have told Luke about us."

"But why would you do that?"

She was the one who swore me to secrecy at the beginning of our affair. She was the one who was so worried about being caught that she wouldn't go swimming with me or be seen anywhere on the hospital grounds with me.

"Well, I didn't name you in particular, if that helps. I just told him that I was having a sexual relationship with one of his doctors." Agatha takes another step towards me and then changes her mind, stays where she is, a few feet inside the door. "Don't worry, he won't guess that it's you. You're too young. You won't fall under suspicion."

"But why would you do that?"

She ignores my question, even though I have asked it twice now.

"He's sending me back to England. Banishing me for my sins. He can't have a wife that strays, not when he's such a bigwig, doing all his important experiments." She smiles weakly, and suddenly I understand everything.

"You're going back to your children," I say.

"Yes."

"It was your plan all along."

"Yes, it was. But I'm sorry. I truly am. It's not that I didn't care for you. I just couldn't bear to be separated from them."

"You used me."

"No." Agatha is forceful in her denial. "Please don't think of it that way, Leonard. It isn't that I used you, but rather that you were able to help me."

ALMOST RIGHT AFTER that distressing meeting, Luke Christiansen comes to the ward to get me. He appears at my office door, looking more official than usual, carrying a clipboard, his breast pocket bristling with pens.

"Flint," he says. There is no trace of sadness or disappointment in his voice over his wife's recently confessed infidelity. "Lead me through your kingdom."

I don't really have a plan for how I am to make the morning unfold in a satisfactory manner, but, thank god, I do have a place to start.

"Let's go to the mattress factory, sir," I say. "There's someone I want you to meet there." I fold up the piece of paper with my false *Results* on it and jam it into my lab coat pocket, in case I need it as backup.

We head outside, down the path behind the hospital,

push open the doors to the mattress factory and hear, immediately, the fast whine of the sewing machines.

I ignore the supervisor, who's waving at me from his office, and lead Dr. Christiansen down the rows of sewing machines to Rusty Kirk. My plan is to introduce them and to explain to Dr. Christiansen how Rusty Kirk is to go to work in the automotive garage starting next week. I'd hoped there would be some discussion between them, that Dr. Christiansen would question Rusty as to his new job, would express his enthusiasm for the venture. I had hoped to actually waste a substantial portion of the morning showing off Rusty Kirk, because I have no other recruits to present to Dr. Christiansen. But none of this happens. What happens instead is that the supervisor, having given up on trying to wave me into his office, chases me down the row of sewing machines and catches me where Dr. Christiansen and I stop in front of Rusty Kirk.

"I've been trying to find you, Dr. Flint," he says. "I've been trying to track you down. We've got a problem."

This is exactly what I don't need to hear.

"What sort of problem?" I ask nervously. I can feel Dr. Christiansen snap to attention beside me at mention of the word "problem."

"Henry Tudor's gone missing. He's run away."

It seems that Henry Tudor has been absent since yesterday after supper. The supervisor did try to find me to tell me this, but couldn't locate me in the dining room on the ward, where I was meant to be. I was, at that time, sitting out with Rabbit Foot Bill in the stables, watching him eat his dinner, trying to calm him down from his agitated state.

"Henry Tudor is a pyromaniac," says Dr. Christiansen. "It is not good to have his whereabouts unknown, not good at all."

"It's downright dangerous in fact," says the supervisor.

They both look at me.

It doesn't seem worthwhile to try to defend myself. I am in the wrong. It is probably my fault that Henry has gone missing. It is certainly my fault that he has been missing for so long without anyone really knowing about it. I listen to Dr. Christiansen and the supervisor discuss whether or not the police should be called as though I was not there, standing between them. Rusty Kirk, I notice, has gone back to his sewing, even though Dr. Christiansen and the supervisor are talking right over the top of his head.

When the discussions have ended and it has been decided that the police should indeed be called, and that there should be a search of the hospital buildings and grounds by the staff, Dr. Christiansen and I walk back outside. The moment the mattress factory doors close behind us, he lets me have it.

"What the fuck is wrong with you, Flint?" he says,

the anger in his voice palpable, spitting the words out at me. "How could you let something like this happen?"

"I don't know, sir." But I do know. I just can't say. I can't tell him about Bill. I must keep that to myself. The way I have been conducting myself with Bill would be an even greater transgression than a missing patient.

"I had my concerns about you from the start," says Dr. Christiansen. "But I always gave you the benefit of the doubt. I thought you were just young and inexperienced, that I could mould you, that working in a place this size could be overwhelming, but you'd step up to the job. I thought the job would make a good doctor out of you. But obviously I was wrong." He runs his hand through his hair and I notice that his hand is shaking. Luke Christiansen is upset after all; perhaps just with me, but perhaps also with Agatha and her earlier devastating news.

"I'm sorry," I say. "I'm overwhelmed by everything. I don't think I am a good doctor."

"No, you're not," says Dr. Christiansen. "Henry Tudor was your patient. You've let him down and possibly put his life in danger and the lives of people in this hospital and the community. He's not a stable man. What if he sets a fire? What if he hurts someone?"

"I'll look for him," I say. "I won't stop looking until I've found him."

"Not good enough." Luke Christiansen lowers his

clipboard, which he's been holding up against his chest like a shield. "I'll have to let you go, Leonard. I can't have you remaining in a position of responsibility over my patients. It's not safe."

I had expected a reprimand, a stiff warning, but I hadn't expected to be fired. It shocks me to think I might have to leave here, and my first thought is, *I can't go. I can't leave Bill.*

"Please, sir," I say. "Just give me another chance. Let me prove to you that I can do this job."

"Too late," says Dr. Christiansen. "I want you out of here." He realizes the harshness of his last remark and his face softens. "It's too bad, Leonard," he says. "I didn't think you were someone who required a paternal hand. I thought you were old enough not to need fatherly strictness, but I can see that I should have been harder on you. I should have given you more supervision. Your failure is also my failure, and letting you go gives me no satisfaction."

I WANDER AROUND my hospital ward in a daze. Most of the men are out working, and there are only a few in the sitting room, playing board games, leafing through magazines. It all looks so benign. I can't believe I couldn't handle my job here. I can't believe that I've been given the weekend to gather my things together and that I'm expected to leave on Monday morning. Where on earth am I going to go?

The men who are on the ward look up as I wander past, their faces registering suspicion and only occasionally recognition. One of them says hello to me, and one of them waves. I haven't helped them at all. I haven't done a single good thing for anyone since I've been here. My failure is not Dr. Christiansen's failure. It is entirely my own.

WILLIAM SCOTT IS in his office when I go to say goodbye.

"I'm leaving," I say from the doorway. "I've been fired. I've come to say goodbye."

"What?"

"I'm a terrible doctor. I don't know why Dr. Christiansen ever hired me in the first place."

But then I remember what he said about thinking he could *mould* me, and about what Agatha said about Luke being a bigwig and doing his important experiments, and I do know why I was hired. The experiments were the important thing, and Luke Christiansen surrounded himself with doctors who would easily go along with what he was doing. I was young, inexperienced, easily malleable. William Scott believed in emancipation, and the LSD experiments could be posited that way, as being about freedom. I don't know the other doctors well, but my guess is that they would all have traits that mesh with Luke Christiansen's professional ambitions. I feel now that I have perhaps been equally used by both husband and wife.

"Why would you be fired?" asks William. "You haven't even been here a season. You must still be on your probationary period."

"I lost Henry Tudor. Or, Henry Tudor became lost while under my care. He's a pyromaniac. And unstable. This whole place could go up in flames any minute."

"Jesus." William takes off his glasses and puts them down on his desk. "It's serious business to lose a patient."

"A fireable offence," I say. "Apparently. No pun intended."

"Maybe you could find him? Maybe if you found him, Christiansen wouldn't let you go?"

"Do you think so?"

I should look for Henry Tudor. I said I would. But I don't really know the man at all and have no sense of where he would go.

"Yes. If you were able to find him, then Christiansen might change his mind about letting you go."

"But where would I start?"

"The ward? It's where he lives. His dormitory room? Use your imagination." William Scott smiles at me. "Don't give up, Leonard."

It seems unreal to me, the fact that I have failed so miserably in my job and that I have been fired, that I will have to leave this place I have barely arrived at, that I will have to leave Bill. This last thought sends a chill through me. How can I be parted from Bill? It was hard enough the first time. It seems impossible now that we've been reunited and are close again.

I leave William's office and head for the dormitory, but when I pass the nurse's station at the end of the hall, I have an idea.

I have seen how LSD can open up someone's thoughts, how it can help patients. Could it not also open up my thoughts and help me in my search for Henry Tudor? Could it not unlock my imagination and make it obvious where my missing patient has gone? If I can find Henry, then perhaps everything can be reversed and I will not have to be separated from Bill.

It's easy to get the nurse on duty to open the drugs cabinet for me. It's too soon yet for anyone to know about my being fired. The nurse just assumes all is as it should be.

I don't remember the exact dosage that patients are given, so I just approximate. I shake some of the liquid LSD into a glass of water, drink it, and then go to my office and sit at my desk, waiting for the drug to take effect.

THE WIND IS up and there are clouds whipping past above my head as I walk down the path from the hospital. I look for Henry Tudor by the fence, through the trees bordering the field, under an overturned wheelbarrow. I imagine him as suddenly small, no bigger than a matchstick, hiding in all manner of places. It makes me smile to think of him as a matchstick. If I found him when he was this small, I could just slip him inside my coat pocket.

Henry is not under the rock my shoe turns over. He is not sitting on top of the dandelion at the side of the road. He is not perched on the back of the bird that flies past my head. He is nowhere and everywhere all at once. I can hear the sound of his matchstick head striking when the wind blows against my coat. I can smell the burning of his matchstick body in the dry grasses that border the cinder path. What if the fire catches and runs all the way to the barn?

"Bill! Bill!" I come bursting through the stable door, all nerves and feeling, but the stables are completely empty. There's not even a horse left in the building.

I go towards Bill's stall, thinking that I will just wait for him there, but all of a sudden my legs are very heavy and walking becomes difficult. I am wading through mud—the effort is that great to pull each foot up and then plant it back down again—and I don't get farther than the bales of hay stacked up against the wall opposite the stalls. Even sinking down to the ground feels like a supreme effort, and it seems to take hours before I am sitting down. It is as though each of my movements has become elastic, just keeps stretching farther and farther out, endlessly, and I am hopelessly chasing after myself in an effort to catch up to what I am doing.

The straw scattered on the floor around my boots appears to be the most splendid gold, each piece shining as brilliantly as a needle of gold. I pass my hand over top of it and can see the gold glowing through my skin. Why did I never notice such riches before? Why couldn't I see the glory that was all around me? I move my leg, slowly, and the straw shifts and glistens, pulls back into a small wave of gold. I move my leg again, and the wave subsides.

I don't know how long I do this for, play with the straw, sit on the floor by the wall of bales. I don't seem to have a sense of time anymore and can't understand it in the old way that I used to understand it. It seems foolish to think I once believed in the regular march of hours. This version of time doesn't move relentlessly along, but billows and collapses. It's not linear, but something that surrounds me.

I don't know how long I am in the stables before Bill comes back. It could have been minutes. It could have been hours. But I hear the drums of the horses' hooves as the team of Percherons enters the building. I want to shout out to Bill, as I did before, but it seems to take tremendous effort just to open my mouth, and after

I do that, I'm not sure how to let the words out from between the bars of my teeth.

The horses see me before Bill does. One of them gives a magnificent snort and shakes his head. Another stamps his foot. I can feel the weight of his foot coming down on the boards as a tiny buzzing all through my body. It's like there are bees in the earth, a whole colony of bees in the earth.

If I hadn't gone out to the stables nothing would have happened. I would have climbed down off the drug after a few hours, returned to my cottage, and packed my belongings. I would have been scared and sullen and still a little high, would have gone out and looked at the river one last time. I might have had the courage to go and say goodbye to Agatha, to wish her well, to wish her a happy reunion with her beloved children. None of that would have been pleasant, but it would have been harmless. I wouldn't have ruined anyone's life. I wouldn't have put anyone at risk.

But we have gone past that now. There is nothing to come but the tragic consequences of my impulsive and irresponsible behaviour.

Bill is behind the horses, guiding them forward into their stalls. He seems to glow as he walks, shed light, and I realize that he is golden, just like the straw.

"Dr. Lenny," he says when he sees me, "are you hurt?"

It seems a funny thing for him to say, and I start to laugh, and then can't stop. It's like my laughter is a machine that turns on itself, goes faster and faster. I can't get off and it's getting hard to breathe, and all of a sudden I'm afraid.

Bill is suddenly on the floor beside me, and I think later about how he knew instinctively what to do. At first I think how remarkable that was, but later it occurs to me that it was simply what he knew. Bill knew madness. He knew the forms it took. He recognized its face. He struggled with the idea of normalcy, with fitting into a world where he didn't belong; but he understood madness. It was his familiar.

Bill gets down on the floor beside me and puts his arms around me. I cower inside the cave of him. I am sobbing now. I'm not sure when the change happened, when my laughter turned to tears, but the sobs rip through my body, each one seeming to fracture more of me. I'm afraid there will be nothing left. I'm afraid that I will be destroyed by my own terrifying sadness.

"Save me," I say to Bill, and he tightens his arms around me. I can smell the horses and the outdoors on his skin. I can feel the cage of his ribs and the scratchy surface of his overalls against my cheek. He mumbles something, but I can't make out the words.

There's a moment when I hang there, in a space between terror and safety, perfectly balanced between those two states. And then everything tips over into terror.

I hear the noise, but I don't know what it is. When I look up, I see the creature bearing down on us. It's a monster. It's black and drips blackness, like it's crawled out of the bottom of a swamp. It's a swamp monster and it has trouble walking on dry land, does a sort of monster shuffle towards me.

I scream, and I don't stop screaming. The monster doesn't slow down, just keeps advancing towards me, and I scream all the louder.

Bill jumps up and I see him reach for something and throw it at the monster. The monster sways a little on his feet and then crashes to the floor and disappears.

WHEN I WAKE up, I'm lying on Bill's bed. He must have carried me in from the main room of the stable and laid me down. I can hear him throwing hay in for the horses, can hear the swish of the hay and the scrape of the fork as it hits the wood of the stalls. I look around. Everything seems returned to normal speed. I look at my hand. It doesn't seem remarkable. I move my head. It's easy to do.

"Hello," I say, and the word comes out without effort.

I struggle up to a sitting position, swing my legs over the side of the cot, and stand up. I walk to the stall door and open it. Bill has respectfully latched it to give me privacy and quiet. I walk out into the stable and I see the body on the floor by the hay bales.

It's Henry Tudor. He's lying on his back. There's a great deal of blood on his shirt, and when I kneel down to check his breathing, I can see that there are four holes in his chest. He's lying perfectly still. I put my shaking hand against his neck to search for a pulse and there isn't one. My head has a sudden sharp pain in it, and I feel as though I'm about to vomit.

I find Bill inside the nearest stall. He swings the pitchfork down to push more hay into the enclosure. He has his back to me. He is tossing the straw into the stalls with a rhythm that is the same as the way field grasses bend to wind, or the way a flame dips and sways, as graceful as a dancer.

"Bill," I say, my voice coming out as a whisper. "Bill, what have you done? Henry Tudor is dead."

Bill turns around and smiles at me. "Lenny," he says, "you were sick, but now you're better."

I take him by the arm and turn him so that he faces the body of Henry Tudor. I can see the blood on the straw where it has been spread out for the horse. I can see blood on the tines of the pitchfork Bill's been using.

"You've killed him," I say. "He's dead. You've killed him."

Bill nods solemnly, and then he turns back to his work. "He had it coming to him," he says.

WEYBURN

—

SASKATCHEWAN
1960

WILLIAM SCOTT MEETS ME IN TOWN. HE comes to the apartment where I live above the restaurant. This has been our arrangement since I was fired from the Weyburn Mental Hospital. William wants to help me, but he can't let it be known to anyone at the hospital that he is helping me. I have left there in disgrace. No one wants to see me come back. Not only did I lose a patient, but I then became, inadvertently, responsible for his death. No greater level of incompetency is possible in someone who has taken the Hippocratic oath.

William and I have decided to do this without LSD, all things considered—the old-fashioned way.

He comes to the apartment three times a week, Monday, Wednesday, and Friday. He comes after work, after dinner on the hospital ward, arriving around nine p.m. and staying until eleven. He borrows Dr. Mortimer's car to drive the small distance into town and waves away my attempts at payment, even though I bring it up at every session. I made many mistakes while at the Weyburn, but for all I did wrong, it seems that maybe I did one thing right. I made a real friend there.

I always leave the apartment door unlocked on those evenings that William Scott comes to see me. I like to sit on the battered old sofa by the window and listen, first for the sound of the car engine shutting off, and then for his footsteps on the stairs. He has a light tread, as though it is nothing for him to walk up several flights of stairs, as though he had all the energy in the world.

Tonight, a Wednesday, he arrives exactly at nine. I hear the soft tap of his feet approaching the apartment, then the squeak of the doorknob turning in its socket.

"Hello," he says cheerfully, entering the apartment.

This is another thing that I have come to rely on from William Scott, now that I know him better. He is always in a good mood. He is always tremendously upbeat. In this way, I can see how he would be a good doctor. Simply being around him would make anyone feel better.

"Hello." I get up from the sofa to go and shake his hand. This is how we greet each other, and how we say goodbye. The formality of it always makes me feel happy.

William means to get to the bottom of my obsession with Bill. That's his term for it—obsession—and I can't say that he is wrong. Even now, I am still anxious to know how Bill is, after he was returned to the penitentiary. Occasionally I ask William Scott to find out, to call the prison and ask after Bill's condition, but he always refuses. He says it would just complicate things, that my problem has always been linked to knowing Bill, and I should know enough not to want to continue this pattern. He believes, although he never comes out and says it directly, that I was abused as a boy by Bill.

We have been at this for several months now. After I was fired from the Weyburn, I didn't know what to do. I didn't want to go back to Montreal, and I couldn't return to my parents' home in Canwood. I couldn't even tell them that I had failed at my first, and perhaps only, job as a psychiatrist. They had been so proud of me when I got accepted into medical school, even though I didn't become what my father called a "real doctor."

At the inquest there was a suggestion that I might face criminal charges for my part in Henry Tudor's death. But Bill had killed before, and it was more convenient for Dr. Christiansen to speak to that, to blame him entirely, and save any scrutiny of his leadership, and of his drug experiments. Christiansen testified that I was trying to stop Bill from killing Tudor, and I got off. "A lucky break," he said to me afterwards, "a second chance."

But nothing about it felt lucky, and as for a second chance, after the inquest, I stayed in town, picked up a job as a dishwasher at a restaurant, and rented this small apartment upstairs. I asked William Scott for help and he agreed and I will stay here, in Weyburn, until he says that I am ready to leave, ready to go back into the larger world. Until he pronounces me cured. Or cured enough.

We sit at the kitchen table. I pour us both a glass of water. William spreads out his papers, uncaps his ball-point pen. There is never much small talk between us. This is not a social visit. Time is limited, so we get right to the point.

"What I still don't understand," says William, "is your unshakable attachment to Bill. It is almost certain he abused you."

"But if he did abuse me, why did I feel no fear towards him?"

I have lain awake nights thinking this very thing. It makes sense that Bill abused me. There was something not right about our relationship. I think I always knew that. But surely if he had abused me, I would have felt afraid of him? And at some point I would have remembered something of the abuse.

"A strange sympathetic response," says William. "You identified with your captor."

"Perhaps."

I certainly did empathize with him. His feelings were my feelings.

"You saw yourself as somehow complicit in your abuse?"

"But I don't have any memories of Bill abusing me," I say. "I just don't believe that he did."

"Why were you so taken with him?"

"I liked his free spirit. I liked how he lived. It was romantic to a young boy. I admired how he behaved around people."

"He was a sociopath," says William. "And he suffered periodic bouts of psychosis."

Sometimes I hate the labels we're meant to attach to people. It seems so bogus, and actually explains nothing of who they are.

"He just didn't give a damn what anyone thought of him," I say. "He was true to himself."

Something suddenly occurs to me.

"I think I even admired the murder," I say. "The first one. The killing of Sam Munroe."

"Why?"

"It was done so recklessly and absolutely."

"Murder often is," says William dryly.

"It's an impulsive act," I say. "Murder is the logical end reach of impulse. I think I can relate to the desire to follow impulse to its conclusion."

"But you have never expressed a desire to kill anyone yourself?" says William.

"But I am a little impulsive myself," I say. "And I think that, given the right circumstances, I could act as Bill acted."

"You could be Bill?"

"Yes."

"You wanted to be Bill?"

"Yes."

William Scott considers for a moment. "That's all well and good," he says, "but it still doesn't entirely explain the attraction."

"There was no one like Bill," I say. "I came from a series of small prairie towns. There was no one as exciting as Bill. He cut a very dramatic figure to a young boy such as myself."

"All right," says William. "I'm willing to see the attraction when you were a boy. But what about when you were a man? What about when you were a working doctor, and you neglected your duties because you were still in thrall to this Bill? How do you explain that?"

I can't explain it.

"I loved him," I say.

"But this was not a harmless sort of love," says William. "This was an obsessive love that caused a great deal of damage to you and those around you. This was a love that resulted in murder."

"It was worse for Bill," I say. "He was incarcerated, all liberties suspended. I was reprimanded and allowed to go on with my life." I feel terrible about this, and guilty for my part in it. Bill was trying to protect me and now he will be locked up forever in prison.

"He was the one who killed. He should have been punished for the act. It is illegal to murder someone."

"But it was my fault he did murder."

"You're protecting him again," says William. "Why do you continue to do this?"

"I love him," I say.

William leans forward. "You didn't use the past tense," he says. "Just then. You said 'love.' Bill is gone. He's in prison. Never to return to your world. It's over."

"But it's not," I say. "It's not over. That's the trouble."

"Describe this love to me."

"What about it?"

"How it felt to you. Back then."

I lean back in the chair and look at the apartment ceiling. There's a large water stain near the window, flaking bits of plaster above my small stove. Sometimes, when I'm cooking, the scales of plaster fall off the ceiling into my frying pan.

"I felt like I wanted to give myself away to Bill," I say. "I wanted to surrender myself to him, to be taken and not returned. I wanted to be free of myself, to fall out of the shape of my life."

"Why did you want to be free of yourself? What were you trying to be free of?"

I think hard. I open myself up to my own subconscious, but nothing occurs to me.

"I don't know."

"I feel we're close," says William. "But whenever I sense we're getting somewhere, you shut down."

"I know."

"Why?"

"I can't answer that."

"Tell me about your relationship with your father," he says.

I know what he's doing. He's found the door bolted and now he's walking around the building looking for an open window.

"It wasn't a close relationship," I say. "He worked long hours. I didn't see all that much of him. I was closer to my mother."

"But you must remember something of the nature of your relationship with him? What sort of things did you do together when you were able to spend time with him?"

I remember the noises of my father. The slam of the door when he came in for supper. The way his sneeze sounded like the bray of a donkey. The reverberations on the kitchen table from the heft of his fist coming down.

"He was a hard man," I say. "He was an angry man. He had to deal with the public in his job and he didn't really like people, so he was often angry at the end of the day when I would see him. Mostly he ignored me, I think, but I do remember that he would sometimes play catch with me. He did teach me how to whittle. Once, we made a wooden flute together."

Later my father snapped the flute in one of his tempers. He snapped the flute and threw it in the fireplace. "Just good for kindling," he said, and at the time, I thought he meant me.

"So, Bill became the father you never had."

"Yes, I suppose so."

"But you chose a man to have a relationship with who didn't know how to relate to people, who chose to take himself out of human society because he couldn't deal with emotional relationships."

"But I was a boy," I say. "I couldn't have known this. To a boy he was a very romantic figure. And he really seemed to care for me."

"He killed for you," says William. "I suppose that's about as caring as you can get. But the relationship, although possibly good for you, wasn't good for him, was it?"

This is what I find so hard to live with, how bad I was for Bill, how good he was to me.

"No, it wasn't."

"So, why didn't you leave him alone when you knew he was getting dependent on you at the hospital, when he was waiting to eat when you did, when he was becoming rather childishly attached to you?"

"I wanted him."

"And what was this wanting? Was it sexual? Was it paternal? Did you want to take care of him? Did you want him to take care of you?"

I can still see Bill sitting on the edge of his bed in the stables at the Weyburn. I can see his handsome face and the shock of black hair that he pushed back with the same fierce swipe that he used to brush a horse's mane.

"It was everything," I say. "All at once. He was everything. As a boy and then now, as a man. Loving him made me love everything else that much more—the song of a bird, the cool strength of the river on my skin—all of it. Because of loving Bill I loved the world with an intensity I haven't felt since."

I stop for a moment, remembering how excited I felt all day at the hospital, thinking I would see Bill that evening, how I would rush off to the stables at every opportunity.

"It wasn't that I loved the world," I say. "It was more that loving Bill made me able to bear the world."

I WORK THE day shift at the restaurant. The busy hours are breakfast and lunch. There's not much custom past five o'clock, and so I finish my working day at six. Before I leave I eat my dinner at the counter, tucking into whatever the special is that day—meatloaf and green beans, hot hamburger sandwich, spaghetti and meatballs. Dessert I take with me on a paper plate, covered carefully over with a veil of plastic wrap.

Scully's Garage is across the road from the diner. Rusty Kirk's day also finishes at six, so when I walk over with the piece of pie, I usually find him outside, straightening up the stacks of oil cans, or coiling the air pressure hose into neat loops. Whenever he sees me approaching, even if I am almost upon him, he stops what he is doing and waves.

"Hey, Doc," he says.

"Hi, Rusty."

I wait until he has finished his chores. Tonight he is cleaning the service station bathrooms, refilling the paper towel dispensers, mopping the floors. I stand just outside the doorway, so as not to block his way, and watch him. He's methodical, wiping down the faucet and taps, arranging the bar of soap just so on the edge of the sink.

"What kind is it, Doc?" he says, his back to me as he swabs the toilet seat with his mop.

"Coconut cream."

"Hot damn!"

The swearing is a new thing for Rusty, learned no doubt from the mechanics he works with at the garage. I should probably be alarmed at this new habit, but it always makes me smile instead. He curses with such joyful emphasis.

After he has finished with the bathrooms, we go inside the automotive bays, to the little space at the back near the office, where Rusty has his cot. Everyone else has left for the day, returning to homes and families. It's like Rusty is the guard dog, I think, as we sit down on his neatly made cot and I hand over the plate of coconut cream pie.

Early on, I stole a fork from the restaurant, and Rusty keeps it washed and ready to use on the upturned crate beside his bed. Next to a small transistor radio, it is the only item there.

"Thanks, Doc." He carefully peels back the plastic wrap and tucks into the slice of pie.

There's something of an echo of Bill in this ritual, and I like sitting on the cot with Rusty, watching him eat the dessert, fork it up with great enthusiasm, smack his lips in satisfaction.

"What do you think?" I ask when he's finished eating.

"Eight." He gives me a thumbs-up and grins.

We have a ranking system for the pies. So far nine has been the highest, for a piece of superb lemon meringue a few weeks ago. The lowest was a four, assigned to a very tart sour cherry pie with a chewy crust that Rusty spat out and didn't finish.

"Here you go, Doc." He solemnly hands the paper plate and piece of plastic wrap back to me. Maybe he thinks that because he receives his piece of pie every evening on an identical paper plate, they can be reused. I don't have the heart to tell him that I just throw the plate and plastic wrap in the trash can outside the garage. He takes such pride in handing this equipment back to me. I want him to have his pride where he can, as I imagine that working at the garage does more to erode his confidence than boost it. I also don't have the heart to tell him that I am no longer his doctor.

"Thanks," I say, putting the plate down beside me. "How did it go today?"

"Oh, pretty good."

"What did you do?"

"Same as usual."

"Nothing different?"

Rusty creases his forehead, thinking.

"Oh yes," he says. "There was something different."

"What was it?"

"A horse. Out by the pumps. A man rode up to the pumps on a white horse and said, 'Fill her up.'" Rusty smiles, remembering. "It was a joke."

"Pretty funny joke," I say.

"The man gave me an apple to feed the horse," says Rusty. "You have to give it this way." He holds out his flat palm towards me. "So the horse doesn't bite your fingers."

"What was the horse's name?"

"Spirit."

"Because it was white."

"I suppose."

I remember the horses in the stable with Bill at the Weyburn, how easily he moved around them and how they were calm with him. I remember the noises of their feet thumping on the ground, how they would shake their heads and snort sometimes. The shudder of the animals was reminiscent of a heart beating—of a heart beating outside the body.

"Tell me about the horse," I say to Rusty. "Everything you can remember."

On Friday night William has come to my apartment with a different agenda than usual. He wants to talk about Agatha Christiansen. I had told him about the affair when we first started our sessions. There seemed no reason to keep any secrets from him, if I genuinely wanted him to help me. But we haven't talked about it since, and I am surprised when he wants to switch from talking about Bill to talking about Agatha.

"Why did you do it," he asks, "if you knew it was wrong?"

"Sleep with her?"

"Yes."

"She approached me."

"But you could have refused?"

"I did refuse at first."

I think of my first sight of Agatha Christiansen,

when she was smoking and hanging streamers in the gymnasium. I had thought she was a little crazy, especially when the streamers were catching fire and she couldn't see a correlation between her cigarette and that fact. But then she had shown me sympathy when I was still smarting over the loss of Amy, and she didn't seem crazy after that.

"She was bold," I say, "and that frightened me off at first."

"But you persisted?"

"Well, she persisted, and I just agreed at some point."

William sits back in his chair. He taps his pen against the tabletop.

"What is it?" I ask.

"I'm thinking."

"Can I ask you something? Off the record?"

"Sure."

"Do you think that Luke Christiansen ever found out that I was the doctor who was sleeping with his wife?"

"I think that he suspected it was you." William puts his pen down. "When he found out how you had lied about other things. That evidence would have established a pattern in his mind. I don't think it would have been hard to make the leap from one thing to another."

I have thought as much myself.

"Do you ever hear from her?" asks William.

"No."

Agatha wouldn't know where to find me even if she did want to get in touch. I hope that she didn't hear about my disastrous run at the hospital, about Henry Tudor's murder and the neglect of my patients. I don't want her to think badly of me. But it's probably much too late for that. She has undoubtedly heard the full account from her husband. They may be geographically and even emotionally distant, but he is sure to have let her know about all of my misdeeds.

"It wasn't ideal," I say. "The fact that she was married. And married to my boss. And maybe it happened because I was so upset about the breakup with Amy."

"But you let it happen when you knew that it wasn't a good idea?"

"Yes. It all happened so quickly, though."

"But you could have slowed it down, Leonard."

"Could I?"

It has never occurred to me that I can slow anything down. I am always going at full tilt, my feet barely touching the ground. I am always racing to catch up to my life, in pursuit of it, running in a zigzag across the field.

William gets up and pours himself a glass of water, comes back to the table and sits down.

"Tell me again how it started," he says.

"She came on to me at the dance, but I saw Dr. Christiansen dancing just behind us and that made me stop. I knew it was wrong. I fled from her advances."

"And then?"

Then there was the darkness rushing up to meet me as I raced across the hospital grounds. There was the moon above the fields, and the shadowy figure of a man out by the stables.

"Then I saw Bill as I was going back to my cottage."

"And pretty soon after that you decided to begin an affair with Agatha Christiansen?"

"Yes."

I can suddenly see where he's going with this.

"Bill again," I say.

"He's like a drug," says William. "All sound judgment is suspended when you are under his influence."

AFTER WILLIAM SCOTT has left, I can't settle. It's too late to pay a visit to Rusty to distract me, and there's no one else I can turn my attention to, so I go for a late-night walk.

The streets of the little town are deserted. All the lights are off in the buildings. I walk to the end of town, out past the last house to where the river cuts through the landscape. The river here is upstream from the Weyburn. If I were to jump in, I could float right past my old cottage, right up to William Scott's door. It's a tempting thought, but I don't jump in. Instead, I walk along the bank, looking at the dark water. In daytime there is a heron that sometimes lifts and lands on this little bit of river, hunting for minnows in the shallows.

It was wrong to have been with Agatha, I can see it now. Not just morally wrong, but also because it was a form of self-sabotage. How would I have been able to prosper at the hospital and be a successful doctor when I was engaged in such a secret and treacherous act? I was hurting myself, and yet I count the times with Agatha Christiansen as happy times. I remember her laughter and the taste of her skin and the look in her eyes that surely was a kind of love—a kind of love for me?

William is right, though, when he equates Agatha with Bill, how one was possible because of my attachment to the other. How one was a result of the other.

I walk along the riverbank and I think of how to unlock the past, of how to figure out the mystery of Rabbit Foot Bill once and for all. For all William Scott's insistent tapping, I have to be the one to actually open the door. I am the one with the answers, even if they seem unavailable right now. But where do I start? What is the best jumping-off point?

I have reached the little stone bridge that signals the end of town. From here the river cuts through farmland and I don't want to follow it out into the stubble of the dark fields. I turn around.

To get to the bottom of my obsession with Rabbit Foot Bill, I think I need to go right back to the first murder.

CANWOOD

—

SASKATCHEWAN
1947

HE TRIAL IS THE BIGGEST THING THAT'S EVER happened in this town. It's all anyone talks about, how Bill killed that poor boy and then went back to cutting the hedge, as though it was nothing.

I am too young to be a trial witness, but the police take a long statement from me, sometimes asking the same questions over and over again.

"What exactly was said between the victim and the accused?"

"Did you see William Dunn push the garden shears into the chest of Sam Munroe?"

It turns out there was another witness to the murder, an adult, so there was less emphasis placed on my account. The other witness was a man living across the street from Mrs. Odegard, who was on his way to the pharmacy and had just stepped out his front door when Sam confronted Bill. He couldn't hear the taunts from Sam, but he did see Bill plunge the clippers into Sam's chest and then pull them out again and continue with his work.

It is this detail, the calm extraction of the shears from Sam Munroe's chest that has set everyone firmly against Bill.

"Why didn't you go for help right away?"

Why didn't I go for help right away? I stood there, watching the blood crawl across the dirt. At some point I must have dropped the water glass, because there were shards of it around my shoes, like pieces of ice from a frozen pond, and I remember thinking of that, of walking out over the ice in winter, of a landscape and a season far removed from this one.

When I finally could speak, after what seemed like ages, with just the *snick snick* of the clippers as the only sound around me, I said, "Bill, I think he's dead. I think you've killed him."

I know I should have run right away for the police or the doctor. I know I should have acted quicker. I don't think I could have stopped Bill from killing Sam. He moved too fast and it happened so swiftly, but I could have acted quicker afterwards.

But when Bill said those words, "He had it coming to him," all I could think was how right he was. Sam Munroe was a bully and he deserved to be treated as badly as he'd treated me. Now he couldn't hurt me anymore. I was glad he was dead.

So, I didn't run for help when it first happened. I only went for the police after the man across the street yelled at me to do so.

But I couldn't explain this when they questioned me. I just said I was too frightened to move, and they believed this. They must have known that I was in shock, and perhaps, too, they thought that I was frightened of being killed by Bill, that if he had murdered one boy, he might be about murdering a second. That would be what they wanted to believe. I couldn't tell them that Bill had done it for me.

When the police questioned me, I wanted to leave out the part where Bill pulled the clippers from the chest of Sam Munroe and set to using them again. Although it made a certain sense to me, knowing Bill as I did, I knew that it would go against him. The police couldn't understand that Bill had to finish a job. He was a hard worker and he liked to work straight through, start at the beginning and end at the end, with no breaks in between. This is partly why I took the water out to him, because he couldn't stop what he was doing long enough to fetch it himself, even if he was thirsty.

I couldn't leave out the part about the shears being removed from the body because the man on his way to the pharmacy had seen it and the police used him as the main witness in the trial. My statement was just meant to support his testimony.

Callous, is what the papers said about that action. *He showed a callous disregard for human life.* My father read this out at the dinner table. He liked to read out the details of the trial, not aware that I knew them all already, that I was there in the courtroom every day. He knew that I had witnessed the murder, and he was there when I gave my statement to the police, but he didn't know about my long association with Bill and thought that I hadn't really been affected by the murder. He always ascribed to me a toughness that I never really possessed.

My father had forbidden me from going to the actual trial, but he couldn't really keep me away. The courthouse was packed, everyone in town was there, and even though children weren't allowed in, my mother's friend Lucy Weber took pity on me and snuck me in with her. I think she thought that I'd been so upset at my young friend's death that it would be good for me to see the murderer brought to justice.

The trial took three days. On the first day they called the lead witness, the man across the street from Mrs. Odegard, who had been on his way to the pharmacy.

"Did you see the accused strike the victim?"

"I did."

"Where did he strike him?"

"In the chest."

"Show the court, if you will, Mr. Melville, where the accused struck the victim, exactly."

There's a murmur in the room when Mr. Melville touches his shirt with his hand, right above where his heart is beating.

"Did the accused strike the victim in the heart, Mr. Melville?"

"Yes, sir."

"And with what did he strike him?"

"A pair of shears."

"Such as one would use for trimming a hedge?"

"Yes, sir. He was trimming a hedge, sir."

"And do you recognize these as being the shears?"

There's a gasp when the clippers are held up for Mr. Melville to identify. Lucy Weber squeezes my hand in excitement or sympathy. I can't quite tell what it is she's feeling on my behalf.

Mr. Melville sways slightly when he sees the clippers, as though he's about to faint. He's a fat man. I can see, even from as far back in the room as Lucy and I are sitting, that his shirt is too tight across his chest. I imagine the clippers embedded in that fat chest, and I wriggle a little on the bench thinking about this. It's hot in the courtroom and the backs of my legs are sticking to the wood of the bench. Lucy grips my hand again. Perhaps she thinks that the sight of the clippers has put the fears into me.

"Yes, sir, those look like the same shears."

"The same shears that the accused used to strike the victim, Sam Munroe, in the chest?"

"Yes, sir."

It goes on all afternoon like this. Each question tightening around Bill, cutting deeper into his flesh and sinew, getting closer to the bone. He sits at a wooden table on the left side of the court with his back to the audience. He is wearing a borrowed blue suit and he sits up very straight. If I crane my neck around the woman in front of me, I can see the back of his head, his thick black hair brushed down for the occasion of his murder trial.

At the end of the first day, Bill is led out, returned to his prison cell. He shuffles along the floor like an old person, and then I realize that he is wearing leg irons. I stand up to get a better look and see the two cuffs of steel around his ankles and the short piece of chain running between them.

I want to wave to Bill or cry out, but he has his head bent, watching the shuffle of his feet across the courtroom floor. He has probably never had his feet in a trap before and he is nervous about how he moves. I don't want to disturb his concentration, so I watch him leave the room, a policeman at each elbow, without letting him know I am here.

On the second day the town doctor is called to the stand to testify.

"Did you examine the body?"

"I did."

"Can you tell the court the nature of the wound that killed Sam Munroe?"

"The left coronary artery had been completely severed. It had been completely severed about one and a half inches from origin."

"Was this a deep wound then?"

"Yes. It was four inches deep."

"A wound caused by the use of considerable force?"

"Yes."

The crown prosecutor holds up the garden shears.

"In your opinion, could the wound have been caused by this pair of garden shears?"

"Yes."

"On examination of the deceased, was this wound the only thing wrong, medically speaking?"

"Some of his organs registered acute shock due to the hemorrhage."

"Which was due to the wound?"

"That is correct."

"To what do you attribute as the cause of this boy's death?"

"Shock caused by fatal hemorrhage."

"And what did you determine to be the exact cause of death?"

"Arterial hemorrhage caused by a stab wound to the heart."

On this second day Lucy Weber and I are closer to

the front of the room. When the prosecutor holds up the clippers, I can see the worn wooden handles polished smooth by the hands of all the people who'd worked them. I can see the dark start of grease on the spring clip near the handle, and a scrape of what looks like dirt on the blades. Blood—it must be blood, not dirt.

"You were one of the first to reach the body. Is this correct, doctor?"

"It is, yes."

"Who was at the site of the body when you arrived?"

"The police constable, Mr. Melville, and the boy who had come to fetch me."

"The boy first went to fetch the constable and then you, is that correct?"

"It is."

The prosecutor turns to the judge and addresses him for a moment.

"The boy in question is one Leonard Flint. We have his statement on record and it supports Mr. Melville's testimony. I hereby submit it as evidence."

"That's you," whispers Lucy Weber, as though I need help recognizing my own name.

I wish the prosecutor hadn't said that about my statement being the same as fat Mr. Melville's. I don't want Bill to think that I turned on him, because I didn't. I just answered what they asked me, but if they hadn't asked me, I wouldn't have told anyone anything. If Mr.

Melville hadn't yelled from across the street at me to get help, I might have gone back inside and poured that second glass of water for Bill.

"Was the boy dead when you arrived, doctor?"

"Yes."

For a moment it seems they are talking about me. I look at the back of Bill's neck. There's a crease of dirt in his skin above his shirt collar, and I can tell by the height and hunch of his shoulders that he's holding them up to protect himself, as though he's expecting blows. I want to climb over all the dull and stupid people in front of me and hurl myself onto his back. I want to wrap my arms tight around him and bury my face into the curve of skin where his neck meets his collarbone, and I want to breathe in the sharp saltiness of him. I want to feel safe again, just one last time.

AT HOME, AT NIGHT, my parents talk of nothing but the trial. My mother feels sorry for Sam Munroe's parents, and my father wishes that Bill would hang for what he did. After supper, my father doesn't go onto the porch to smoke, but lingers around the kitchen while my mother washes the dishes. He likes to have me recount the murder, over and over again, until he tires of this and I can excuse myself and go to do homework in my room. I am lucky that his job at the train station makes it impossible for him to attend the trial, and I am lucky, too, that my mother feels so disturbed by Sam's violent death that to go to the courthouse would be just too upsetting. She relies on Lucy Weber's recounting of events at the end of each day to keep her informed.

From my bedroom I can hear my parents talking down the hall. My father likes to retell my version of the murder and then pronounce on it. Every time he gets to the part about Bill stabbing Sam in the heart with the shears, my mother says, "Don't. Please don't," as though he is about to raise the shears himself and plunge them through the wall of her chest.

ON THE THIRD and last day of the trial, Bill is called to take the stand. There is nothing worse for a man who doesn't like to talk than being made to do so, and I cringe when I see how nervous Bill is inside the little wooden box. He keeps darting his head from side to side and pulling on the collar of his borrowed suit. All the nervous movement makes him look crazy.

Lucy Weber and I are sitting in the third row. We got here early and lined up outside to get a good seat. This is the final day of the trial and the courtroom is filled. This is the day when the judgment is meant to be coming down, and no one wants to miss it.

The witness box is raised up on a little stage beside

the judge's bench, and I have a good view of Bill. I don't like how scared he seems, how he fidgets inside the suit like he's got the pox.

"He looks so guilty," says Lucy. "He's gone all twitchy with it."

The prosecutor rises to his feet. "William Dunn, can you recount for the court what happened on the afternoon of June 17?"

Bill just looks nervously about. It's like he doesn't know they're talking to him, that they expect an answer from him.

"Please answer the question, Mr. Dunn."

"What?"

"Where were you on the afternoon of June 17?"

"Cutting the hedge for the missus Odegard."

"Were you alone?"

"Yes."

I like that Bill is protecting me, although it's pointless, as the judge already knows from my statement that I was there.

"Mr. Dunn, there was a boy there too, was there not?"

"No."

"A one Leonard Flint?"

"No."

Everyone knows that Bill is lying. Parts of my statement have been read out to the court. People have heard the testimony of Mr. Melville, who recounted seeing me standing by the hedge, talking to Bill. I dig my nails into my wrists to prevent myself from crying out for Bill to stop lying. It is making everything worse for him if he denies what everyone else knows to be true.

The prosecutor waves his hands in exasperation, as though he's dismissing Bill entirely.

"Did you kill Sam Munroe?"

Bill has his head bowed and is mumbling something.

"I can't hear you, Mr. Dunn."

There's more mumbling.

"What?"

Bill suddenly raises his head and looks out at the prosecutor. His fidgeting has stopped. He's angry now. I can tell that he's angry now, because he has a calmness and strength about him.

"He had it coming to him," he says.

After that it's all over for Bill. It's the last clear thing he says and he just keeps on saying it. No matter what else the prosecutor asks him, all he answers is that Sam "had it coming to him." There really is nothing else to do but find him guilty. He is guilty. I have to keep reminding myself that he is guilty, because I just feel so sorry for him up on the stand, getting pestered with all the lawyer questions.

The verdict is manslaughter and the sentence is life in the Prince Albert Penitentiary.

"Well, that's justice done," says Lucy Weber, snapping the clip on her purse shut with satisfaction.

Everyone is on their feet preparing to leave the courthouse. I can't see for all the moving arms and legs, and I am frantic to find Bill before he is taken from the room.

I burst through the people in front of me, climb up on the benches and down again, until I am on the floor of the courtroom, right in front of Bill and the two policemen who are preparing to lead him out of the room.

"Bill!" I say, and I rush forward to touch him, but one of the policemen swats me back.

Bill looks down at me. He has a wild look in his eyes, wild and unfocused, like he's been out in the sun all day and has suddenly come indoors and can't adjust to the change in light.

I want to tell him not to worry, but that's stupid. I want him to tell me not to worry, but that's stupider still. I strain against the barrier of the policeman's arm, and all of a sudden, Bill's eyes clear and he looks at me like he knows me.

"See to my dogs," he says. "Will you go and see to my dogs?"

"I will."

The policemen have started Bill moving again and I call out to him when he's at the door of the courtroom.

"I'll take care of the dogs, Bill. I'll look after them. Don't worry. You don't have to worry."

Bill turns when he hears me yelling this and he nods his head to show he's understood me, that he trusts I will do what he needs me to do. Then he is pushed through the door and the last I see of him is the slope of one blue-suited shoulder as he's jostled out of the courtroom and into the hallway.

LUCY WEBER COMES to my house that night to tell my mother about the final day of the trial. They sit out together on the front porch drinking iced tea. I try to sit with them for a while, but my mother banishes me to my bedroom.

"You've had enough of this," she says. "It's too much for a child."

I lie on my bed, listening to the flutter of their voices through the wall. I can't hear the words, but the murmur is comforting, like wind through the prairie grass.

My father is gone. He's visiting another station master farther up the line and won't be home for a day or so. He likes to say that these visits are about his work, but my mother tells me the truth, that he likes to go away from home so that he can "drink without guilt." He always comes back nicer than when he left, so we never mind his absences.

After a while, I can hear the creak of the porch chairs as the women get up from them, the click of the screen door, and one set of footsteps inside the house. Lucy Weber must have left and my mother has come in to get ready for bed. I listen to her footsteps get fainter as she goes into the bedroom she shares with my father, on the opposite side of the building.

There's a timid knocking at my window, and I leap off my bed and wrestle the shuddery pane up its frame. It's Lucy Weber, standing in the roses.

"I just wanted to come and say goodbye," she says.

"Thank you for not blabbing about me coming to the trial with you," I say.

"It was my pleasure to take you," she says. "I enjoyed your company. And . . ." She hesitates for a moment and then reaches through the window and squeezes my hand. "I wanted to do something nice for you, Leonard. I'm no fool. I know what kind of man your father is."

CANWOOD

—

SASKATCHEWAN
1970

Y MOTHER MEETS ME AT THE STATION.

"Pleasant journey?" she asks.

"Good enough."

She presses herself against me, less of a hug than the way a dragonfly lights on skin, how it rests for a moment and then pushes back off into the air it came from.

I follow her out to the dusty, battered, green Ford.

"You still have the truck," I say, lifting my suitcase over the side and into the bed, where it sits beside a spare tire and a tangle of wire.

"It still runs," she says. "So, why not?" She shrugs and gets in, hauling herself into the cab by the steering wheel because she's not tall enough to step up easily into the truck.

We drive in silence, the prairie landscape unspooling before us. I have forgotten the grandeur of it, how it is vast like an ocean. Off in the distance there is a column of grey, rain coming down on some other patch of earth, some other community. I can't tell if the storm is moving towards us or moving away. It is one of the miracles of the prairie landscape that you can watch rain approaching hours before it arrives.

At the house, my mother lurches the truck to a stop in front of the porch.

"You can have your old room," she says when I come into the front hall with my luggage. "It's much the same. I was waiting . . ." She stops because we both know what she is going to say next and there's no point.

"Okay." I carry my suitcase down the hall.

"Tea?" she calls from the kitchen.

"Sure."

My bedroom is as I remember it—the single bed by the window, simple dresser against one wall, white wooden chair at the end of the bed. Sometimes I would sit in that chair and look out the window, past the rose bushes, to the flat scrape of fields. On a windy day, the dust would rise from the fields like a veil. The immensity of the landscape made it feel as though I could see everything coming from far away, not merely the weather. Even words seemed to float towards me before they'd been uttered.

Now I live in Toronto, a city of trees and ravines, streetcars and roads—the landscape interrupted every few feet. The only thing in that landscape that is remotely like anything in this one is the lake, the flat blue tilt of it at the southern end of the city, cut off from my neighbourhood by a tangle of expressways.

I put my suitcase on the bed and go back out to the

kitchen. My mother has made tea in a couple of mugs and we take them out to drink on the porch.

"Thank you for coming," she says.

"You don't need to thank me." He was my father, after all. It feels necessary to come home for his funeral.

"What will happen to the house?" I ask. A station master is given a house with the job, but now that my father is dead, there will be a new station master in Canwood.

"I'll have to go."

"Soon?"

"They'll allow me a few months." My mother puts her mug of tea down on the arm of her chair. I notice that her hand shakes a little now. "Don't worry. I have a little put aside. I'm going to move into town. Maybe rent a little house near Lucy Weber. You remember her?"

"Yes. I remember Lucy Weber very clearly in fact. She was always very kind to me."

I think of the last time I saw Lucy Weber, how she held on to my hand through the window, how her words had shocked me because it was the first time that I had heard someone speak out against my father.

"She took me to the trial," I say. "When Bill was charged with murder."

"That vagrant you used to pester?"

"He wasn't a vagrant. He just had a different way of living his life."

"Don't get upset, Leonard." My mother pats my hand.

I pull mine away.

"I should go and unpack," I say, and get up abruptly and go into the house.

In my old room I sit down on the small single bed. The mattress is soft and I can feel the springs digging into the underside of my thighs. It might be the same mattress from my childhood, and probably no one has slept on it since then. There were never many visitors to our house when I was young, and certainly none that ever stayed overnight. My parents didn't have many friends, and no relations were near enough to visit. I touch the raised crocheted roses on the bedspread. Once bright red, they are faded pink from age, from the sun angling in from the window, day after day, year after year.

There's a timid knock on the bedroom door.

"Leonard?"

"I'm fine."

In the silence that follows, I wait for my mother's footsteps to retreat back down the hallway, but she stands outside the closed door for what seems an unbelievably long time.

"I'm fine," I say again, and only then do I hear her weary shuffle down the length of hallway towards the kitchen.

When William Scott and I finally got to the bottom of my obsession with Bill, he wanted me to write a letter to my mother. He thought that I needed to forgive her.

It was the only way to truly move forward, he said. But I couldn't write that letter. Every time I started, every time I sat at the kitchen table in my apartment above the restaurant in Weyburn and put *Dear Mom* at the top of a piece of paper, I couldn't think of what to say next. My palms would sweat and I would get dizzy, and there seemed to be no stream of words that I could enter that would wash away the way I felt.

I spent a year talking with William Scott three days a week. I still see him occasionally. After the Weyburn was emptied of patients and closed for good, he took a job in Ontario. He works at a clinic in Markham, outside of Toronto. Sometimes we'll talk in the morning, when I'm at the lab on an early shift and before his day has officially begun. I retrained after my failure at the mental hospital and work in a lab for infectious diseases now. No more patients, just microscopes and slides. I have moved from the doctoring side of the equation to the scientific side. It's probably where I belonged all along. I am more at home among blood cultures than human beings.

I open my suitcase and close it again. I don't really want to unpack, prefer to keep everything feeling temporary, like I could leave at any moment. But I walk over to the dresser and open all the drawers anyway. The wood smells like mothballs. In the bottom drawer is a folded bolt of fabric. I recognize the tiny repeating yellow primroses from the curtains above the kitchen sink.

Childhood seems remote, like a landscape seen from the window of a speeding car, blurry and inaccessible. I can put my hand on the faded roses of the bedspread, or on the worn grooved wood on top of the dresser, on this folded length of cloth, but I'm not feeling anything of my former life.

I want to call William Scott and ask him what to do, but he's in the middle of his workday, and the only phone in this house is in the kitchen. My mother would be able to hear every word I spoke into the receiver.

So, there's nothing to be done, and I go back out into the hallway and start walking towards the kitchen. Even though I can't call William Scott to ask for his advice, I know what it would most likely be. *Keep moving forward, Leonard*, he would say. *Don't let yourself fall backwards.*

My mother is sitting at the table, smoking.

"I thought you gave that up," I say.

"It's just for my nerves," she says, not looking at me, tapping her long ash into the green glass ashtray in front of her. I can see how much older she is now, how her cheeks are furrowed and the skin around her eyes is lined. It makes me a little sad to think of her as an old woman. But then she was always careworn, always seemed a bit like an old woman, even when she was young.

The green ashtray is in the shape of a fish. The cigarette butts covering the inside of it look like scales patterning the side of the glittering glass creature. I suddenly have a memory of noise and lights, the creak of carnival music from the sports field outside of town.

"Did I give you that ashtray?" I ask.

"You won it at the sideshow," says my mother. "At the shooting range, I think."

"Yes, that's right."

I can remember the weight of the gun in my hands, the spinning targets, the wooden shelves overflowing with their bounty of prizes. Was this before or after the murder? Before, I think, when I was still relatively happy.

"You've kept it all this time."

My mother looks up at me then. I can see her eyes are bright with tears, that she's been crying.

"Why wouldn't I keep it?" she says. "It was a present from my son."

WE EAT DINNER mostly in silence, just the knocking of the cutlery against the plates. I can hear the click of insects outside the kitchen window in the waning summer heat.

It's all so familiar—the sound of the insects, the mismatched silverware, the dinner plates with sheaves of wheat—and yet I feel removed from all of it, as though I'm watching from somewhere outside of myself. I look over at the refrigerator, which has shuddered and knocked itself back into life—another sound I am relentlessly familiar with—and realize, from my days of working with William Scott, that I'm showing signs of dissociative behaviour.

My mother has made me a pie for dessert.

"Saskatoons," she says, slicing through the crust and revealing the firm purple berries underneath. "I thought you might have a hankering for them, after living in the city."

"Thank you."

I take the plate of pie she passes to me across the table.

Once, when I tried to explain the Saskatoon berry to my wife, Maggie, I said it was like a meaty blueberry. That was the closest I could come to describing what it was like, but really that wasn't close enough. The Saskatoon retains its shape when baked, doesn't mush up like other berries or leak flavour in the cooking. The juice is the most beautiful purplish red, like a combination of grapes and blood. I used to pick and eat loads of the berries when I was a child, stuffing my face with them from the shrubs in the gullies at the base of Sugar Hill.

"It's delicious," I say, and I don't say no when my mother cuts me a second piece of pie after I have finished my first.

And then, just when I am starting to relax, when eating the pie and thinking of the Saskatoons has made me feel like myself again, I can see the phantom bulk of my father passing behind my mother's chair, can see how she flinched every time he crossed behind her and was out of sight, because often he would hit her on his way to the fridge to get a beer, club her on the side of her head with an open hand and enough force to spill her onto the floor.

"What's the matter?" asks my mother.

My hand with the fork is poised above the wedge of pie.

"Nothing. I'm just not hungry anymore. I think I've had enough to eat."

Through the kitchen window the sun rolls back behind the fields and the crickets begin in the yard. I can hear them tuning up under the rose bushes.

I push the plate away from me. My mother pushes it gently, but insistently, back.

"Finish your pie, son," she says. "It's always best on the day it was made. It won't be nearly as good by tomorrow."

After supper I excuse myself by saying that I'm tired from the journey, go into my bedroom, and close the door. I lie down on my bed, fully clothed, and shut off the bedside lamp. The room is so dark that I cannot see my hand in front of my face. I switch the lamp back on.

I would never hear him coming. That was part of it, the surprise attack. He was a big man, but he could creep down the hallway as silently as a cat. I wouldn't hear him turning the doorknob or folding the door carefully back against the wall. He would cross the floor while I slept, and I only woke when he was right there beside the bed, when he reached down and grabbed me, shook me from the shrouds of sleep.

I get out of bed and take the chair and jam it under the doorknob. But then I remember that I did this once when I was a child and he surprised me by coming through the bedroom window.

I remove the chair out from under the doorknob and carry it back to the window. Then I lift the window in its sash and sit in the chair, lean my head out into the night, inhale the cool inrush of air, the scent of grass and road tar.

Once, I sat here like this as a boy, with my head out the window, and I watched as my father chased my mother around the house. She was barefoot but running hard, running over the stones and the dirt as though they were the softest grass. She made a grunting noise when she ran, because she was trying to go her fastest and it was taking everything out of her. No use, though, as he caught her near the downspout and dragged her out into the field. And all through that, I just sat still on the chair at the window. What I felt in that moment was not fear, but relief that it was my mother he was after and not me.

I don't remember moving from the window or falling asleep, but when I wake it's the next day. The bedside lamp glows dimly in the morning light and I'm sprawled across the single bed with all my clothes still on, lying on top of the covers. I feel foolish and grateful at the same time.

It's the day of the funeral. I should have hung my suit up when I arrived yesterday instead of leaving it folded in my suitcase. But when I haul it out, it's not too crumpled. I lay the shirt and jacket on the bed and smooth them down carefully with the flat of my hand.

My mother is standing by the sink, looking out the window and drinking a cup of coffee. She's wearing her one good dress—the same one good dress that I recognize from my childhood. Her hair is up.

"Beautiful day," she says, her back still turned to me.

I pour myself some coffee from the pot on the stove and go to stand beside her at the window.

"Your roses are looking good this year."

"I've had more time for them," she says. "It's always good to deadhead right after they bloom."

"Yes, they look tidier."

"I meant to cut you a spray for your room before you got here."

"No mind."

"Let me do it now. Before I forget and the day gets away from us."

Before I can say anything to stop her, my mother is out in the yard with a pair of scissors, snipping the heads off the yellow roses under the kitchen window. Her bent body looks vulnerable, like a child, and I can see that her hair is thinning around the crown.

She comes back inside with a small bouquet, holds them up for me to smell. I drop my face towards them, but the sweet, perfumed musk makes me suddenly nauseous. I sway on my feet, reach out for the kitchen counter to steady myself.

"What's the matter?" asks my mother.

"Nothing. I'm just going to go and get some air," I say. "I'll meet you out by the truck."

I walk slowly around the house until I'm at the back by the bed of roses. The pale yellow flowers grow along the wall of the house and twine around the door of the root cellar.

When my father would grab me out of sleep, he would take me outside to beat me, so my mother wouldn't hear. He would drag me around to the back of the house, to this place by the roses and the root cellar. It was on the opposite side of the house to the room where he slept with my mother, and in those days she took something every night so she could sleep. I remember the army of pill bottles lined up in the bathroom medicine cabinet.

On the better nights, my father would hit me until I fell, and then, while I lay on the ground, the scent of the roses drifting around me, he would put the boots to me.

On the worst nights, my father would beat me and then throw me into the root cellar and leave me there until morning. He must have weighted the door with rocks or logs, because it was impossible to budge from the inside, even though I pushed against it with everything I had in my panic to get out.

He can't hurt you now, William Scott would say if he were here, but I am shaking and still nauseous. Memory is a lesser substitute for my father's brutality, but it is still terrifying.

I slowly raise the wooden cover on the root cellar, lift it open, lean it back on its hinge against the wall of the house, and climb down the rickety wooden ladder of a staircase.

I can't, even now, think of a reason why I was beaten. In all honesty, it never really seemed to be about me at all. Instead it was about quelling my father's rage. He had a rage that seemed to simmer for a while and then it had to boil over, by necessity. The beating put everything back on simmer and made him calm and human again. Until the next time.

It was night, so I must be hit. It was Wednesday, so I must be hit. The world had treated my father unfairly, so I must be hit. He was a failure, so I must be hit. It had rained for three weeks straight, or it hadn't rained all summer and the garden was ruined, so I must be hit.

The smell of the cellar is the smell of darkness, sharp and damp and sweetened with decay. It is what blood tastes like, that smell.

I would lie curled up tight in the hole of the root cellar. I was always cold in there and my body hurt from the beating. I curled up tight for warmth and to avoid touching the salamanders that lived in that dark place. Mud puppies, they were called, and they were sticky and cool when they scrabbled over my skin. A frightening lizard with the comforting name of a pet.

I have been inside the earth. I have closed my eyes and opened them, and in the blackness my own hand in front of my face is impossible to see. I have been invisible. I have become this darkness I have entered—a darkness that is soft and cool and smells of mice and old potatoes.

My mother is standing outside the truck when I come around the side of the house.

"Where have you been?" she asks. "I went out back and couldn't see you." She brushes down the front of my suit jacket. "You're covered in cobwebs. You have dust in your hair."

"I was down in the root cellar."

My mother gives me a strange look.

"Why would you want to go down there?"

I shrug and get into the truck.

We drive along the dusty road, past one quarter section and then another. The fields humming by, wheat changing to rapeseed and then to flax, a line of poplars or length of dirt road segmenting one field from the next. I've always liked the blue of the flax when the flower is in bloom. It's a blue like smoke. When a whole field of flax moves in the wind, it has the creep of water.

My father was a godless man, but the funeral is at the Presbyterian church in the centre of town.

"Where else?" says my mother as she rocks the truck to a stop beside the curb. "We can't very well put him in the yard."

Through the double oak doors, the church smells like rotting lilies. Probably remnants from the last funeral, like a stain left on the air. There are no flowers here today for my father. My mother didn't bring a spray of yellow roses to put on his coffin, and who would want to buy him a wreath? Certainly not me. He had a few drinking friends up and down the rail line, but no one in Canwood who was more than a nodding acquaintance. My father had a suspicious view of his fellow humans, always thought he was being cheated or would be cheated, that people were nothing more than opportunistic dogs, forever on the make.

I sit beside my mother in the front row. A few people wander into the church. I don't turn around to see who they are, and perhaps they're not even there for the funeral, but have wandered in by accident, to enjoy the cool quiet of the church interior. But then someone deliberately enters the pew behind us and I feel a hand on my shoulder.

"Hello, Leonard."

It's Lucy Weber. She looks older but the same. I am filled with happiness at the sight of her.

"Hello, Miss Weber."

She squeezes my shoulder and I put up a hand to cover hers. Her skin is dry and papery.

The box that holds the body of my father sits beside the altar. When the minister says the requisite words for the service, he has to look down at the sheet of paper in front of him to get the name of my father right.

Afterwards, we traipse out to the gravesite for the burial. It's hot out now and the minister sweats through his vestments as he sprinkles the words of God down on the wooden box where my father will be trapped for all eternity.

My mother and I stand side by side, not touching, while the coffin is lowered into the sleeve of earth. There are bits of root and small stones studding the walls of the hole. The squawk of a magpie comes from a nearby tree.

"Amen," says Lucy Weber firmly when the minister has stopped speaking.

The coffin has reached the bottom of the grave. It wobbles to a stop and then the green canvas straps that lowered it are winched slowly up to the surface.

"Come back to mine," says Lucy Weber to my mother and me. "I have some lunch laid on for you."

As we walk away I can hear the sound of the dirt being shovelled into the hole. It sounds like rain, like a hard rain driving against a window, like the kind of rain we sometimes had in summer when I was a boy. I suddenly miss my father, and I want to turn back to the grave, but Lucy Weber has me firmly by the elbow, guiding me towards the parking lot.

I'm glad we're going back to Lucy's. It saves me from the inevitable crawl of small talk with my mother. We follow Lucy's white car through the cemetery gates, my mother wrestling the gears of the truck into their sockets, and me staring out the window at the granite markers, the etch of birth and death dates, the sprigs of bright plastic flowers.

"Will you get him a headstone?" I ask my mother.

"I probably owe him that," she says. "But it will be a small one."

Lucy's bungalow is cheerful, packed with furniture and knick-knacks, plants on all the window ledges. It is the opposite of my parents' stark farmhouse, with only my mother's few nice things to brighten the space.

"I like to have greenery in winter," says Lucy as I run my finger along the frond of a potted fern. "It helps dispel the gloom."

She disappears into the kitchen to fetch the lunch.

My mother kicks off her shoes, curls up on the couch with an ease that she never displays in her own house.

"I like it here," I say.

"Yes," she says. "I do too. It's an oasis."

Lucy reappears bearing a tray full of sandwiches with their crusts cut off and a pitcher of iced tea. She sets both down on the coffee table, shoving piles of books out of the way to make room.

"It's cozier to eat in here," she says. "So let's do that. I'll just go and get the plates and glasses." She trots off back to the kitchen.

The sandwiches are arranged in a wheel on the plate. Salmon paste, and ham and mustard, and what looks like cream cheese studded with chopped-up dill pickle.

"They look so nice," my mother calls out. "You shouldn't have gone to so much trouble."

"Nonsense." Lucy is back again, puts three glasses down on the table and hands us each a plate and paper napkin. "It's the least I can do." She pours the iced tea. "I wanted to help."

I'm hungrier than I knew, fill my plate three times with sandwiches, down the iced tea in a series of gulps.

Lucy refills my glass.

"It's good to see you looking so well, Leonard," she says.

"It's good to see you too," I say.

I have not forgotten her kindness to me, and I want

to tell her that, but it seems impossible to do with my mother here. So it is a relief when, after a small plate of food, my mother announces that she is tired and should probably go home to have a rest.

"Leonard," says Lucy as my mother stands up, slips her shoes back on, smooths down the front of her one good dress, "why don't you stay for a bit? We can get caught up. I can drive him back," she says.

"All right." My mother makes no protest, and I realize that it is probably just as much of a strain for her to be with me as it is for me to be with her. Perhaps it is not just me who is making small talk?

I watch from the window as she walks down the flagstone path, climbs up slowly into the truck, and backs down the driveway.

Lucy comes and stands beside me at the window.

"It was good of you to come back for her," she says.

"But I didn't come back for her," I say. "I came home to make sure that he's really dead."

"Ah." Lucy is quiet for a moment. "It's hard on your mother," she says after a pause, "that you have been so distant."

I don't know if she means the geographical distance or my emotional distance, although they might as well be one and the same at this point. I haven't been back to see my mother since my daughter was born six years ago.

"My father was a terrible man," I say. "A real fucking bastard."

"I know."

"And she never left him. After everything he did. To her. And to me. She just stayed and stayed."

"She tried to leave. Several times."

"I don't think so."

"She did," says Lucy Weber. "Trust me. But where was she to go? She had no money of her own. She couldn't get far. And each time she left, he found her out and forced her back. I hid her here once, and he kicked in my front door."

"You should have called the police then."

"Leonard," says Lucy, "you want it to be simple, and it's not simple." She leads me back to the couch and we sit down together.

"But it is simple," I say. "He was a monster and she let it happen."

"Did she?"

I think of my mother cowering in the corner of the kitchen, her arms over her head in a useless attempt to ward off the blows. I think of her kneeling beside my bed in the mornings after I had been beaten, wiping the dried blood from my face with a washcloth, her tears falling on my swollen eyelids.

"No," I say. "I guess not. I guess it happened to both of us."

Lucy puts her hand over mine.

"I'm sorry," she says. "I should have done more."

"It's not your fault."

We're quiet for a moment.

"But why did it happen?" I ask.

Because I don't understand why my father was so violent to his family, to those he was supposed to love.

"I remember when the men got off the train," Lucy says.

"What men?"

"Your father. Bill Dunn. How they came home still in their uniforms, carrying their kit bags. How they walked off that train, fresh from the battlefields of Europe, and they were expected to go straight back into their lives after having been gone all that time. After having fought and killed and suffered. They were expected to just pick up where they had left off."

I knew that my father had been in the war, but he had never talked about it. He always evaded the subject if I questioned him about those years. But I didn't know that Bill had also been a soldier.

"How could they go on as normal?" says Lucy. "After all they had seen and done? I didn't have this opinion at the time, but I think now that Bill was the smarter man. He knew enough to take himself out of society, to remove himself from his family."

"Bill didn't have a family."

"Oh yes he did, Leonard," says Lucy. "But he didn't stay with them. He came home and right away he went to live rough. He might have spent a week or two with his wife and children, that's all. Then he left, and then they left, and I doubt he ever saw them again."

"He had children?"

"Three children. Two bigger girls and a young boy. His wife took them back east, to where her family were living. Trudy, I think that was her name. She had the bluest eyes. Funny what you remember of a person. I don't recall much else about her, but I remember those piercing blue eyes."

It has never occurred to me that Bill had a family, that he had children. He seemed such a singular figure, striding through the prairie landscape of my childhood.

"But he never told me he had children?"

"Leonard, why would he have told you anything? You were a child yourself when you knew him."

Lucy doesn't know about my later, fateful encounter with Bill. She doesn't know that I was fired from my job at the Weyburn, or that Bill was there, or that he killed Henry Tudor. I'm not about to bring it up now. It's too long and sad a story, how Bill came back into my life and what happened to him because of our association.

"I do think that Bill got it right," says Lucy. "Even though, at the time, and along with everyone else in town, I thought he was cruel to abandon his family. But he knew that he was damaged from the war, and he knew enough to keep that damage from his wife and children. Especially his children." She pauses. "I'm sorry for what happened to you, Leonard, and I do wish I had been able to do more for you and your mother."

"You were always nice to me," I say. "That mattered to me a lot."

We're quiet again for a short while. I'm trying to get my head around Bill having had a family, having had a wife and children. Especially children. What would it have been like for him to make a decision to leave them? Now that I have a daughter, I know how devastating it would feel to never see her again.

"But when you talk about my father and the damage caused by the war, are you excusing him?" I ask Lucy after a few minutes. "Because I don't think I can do that, no matter what happened to him in the battlefield, or how hard it was to adjust to family life when he got home."

"I'm not excusing him," says Lucy. "There is no excuse for what he did to you and to Janet. I just wanted to explain some of the background of his life to you, give you information that you might not have otherwise known."

I was seven when my father went to war. We lived in Prince Albert then, a bigger place than Canwood. I remember clinging to his pant leg at the train station, and how he spun me around before he hugged me good-bye. He held on to my arms and twirled me around and it felt like I was flying.

I can understand that he was a different man before the war, because I have those memories to hold against the ones when he returned.

"Did Bill and my father know each other in the war then?" I ask.

"They were in the same regiment," Lucy says. "That's why they were both on the same train coming home. The men from that regiment would have travelled back from Europe together."

There would have been weeks of travel. First the troop ship from Southampton to Montreal. Then a train to Toronto. And finally the long train ride from there to Saskatchewan. All that time my father and Bill would have spent talking and being around each other. They might have got drunk together, or played cards, or simply looked out the window and made small talk. One might have fallen asleep with his head on the other one's shoulder. They were most likely good acquaintances, or even friends. At the very least, having served together and being from the same place, they would have known each other very well.

I think of how closely my father paid attention to Bill's trial for the murder of Sam Munroe, how he liked to recount the details from the newspaper to my mother at night, how he liked to quiz me about the murder. He never let on that he knew Bill or that they had served in the war together. Was he ashamed of their association? Did he think himself the better man for resuming his life, while Bill had abandoned his family and become the local tramp? Did this make my father feel superior? Did he even know what sort of person he really was?

"I wonder what ever happened to Bill Dunn?" Lucy says. "If he's still in that prison."

"He died."

"How do you know?"

"I kept track of him."

Bill died the year after he was taken into custody for the murder of Henry Tudor and returned to the penitentiary. I'm not sure how he died, as no one would give me that information when I inquired after him, but I do know that he did die.

"That's a real shame," says Lucy.

"Yes," I say. "It truly is."

I stay at Lucy Weber's for a while longer. She wants to drive me back to my mother's, but I wave away her offer and say that I could do with the walk. It's probably five miles, but I am not bothered. When I was a boy I could cover twice that distance in a day. My feet would fly over the earth, barely touching down.

It's the end of summer and the light leans on the horizon as though it's tired. The months of green and heat are shutting down, and I can already see the line that winter will take across the fields.

I start out on the road back towards my parents' house and then I change my mind.

I FIND MY way back to Sugar Hill by instinct. I could probably do it with my eyes shut.

There's a road there now. The hill is the one high place in the area and must be popular with walkers and people out for a Sunday picnic. The hill is taller than I remember, and full of small trees and a patchwork of scrub. There's a path that switchbacks to the top, well worn from boots and bikes. Before I start up the path, I look around the base of the hill for signs of Bill's old house. Nothing is visible. Whatever used to be there has long since filled in and grown over. There's no evidence that anyone ever lived inside Sugar Hill.

I get down on my hands and knees and scrabble around in the grass and dirt. Sometimes it feels like I made up Bill's life here, that it was all some sort of child-hood mirage. But I uncover a small cache of bones in a depression of earth, and they look like rabbit bones to me. And by the beginning of the path to the hilltop is a rose bush, huge and tangled, but still recognizable as a cultivated rose, not a wild one. Along the path there are a few raspberry canes, and the feathery tops of asparagus plants gone to seed.

The climb is a hard one and I have to keep stopping to catch my breath. I remove my suit jacket, and then my tie, stuff it in my trouser pocket. When I get to the top, I stand on a bare patch of hillside, looking down. There's a charred piece of earth near my feet, where people have made a fire. There are a few beer bottles and a couple of candy wrappers on the ground. In the distance are the familiar rectangles of the farm fields, the little bit of stitching below them that is the rail line. Strung out in a line along the rail tracks, the grain elevators are solid blocks of red and brown.

I miss Bill, standing on top of Sugar Hill. I miss him with an ache that whistles through my body. All I have left to remember him by are the three rabbits' feet lined up on the windowsill of my daughter's bedroom at home in Toronto. Sarah likes to rub the softness of the fur against her face, or pretend that the feet are real rabbits, that they are her pets. Sometimes I take them down from the windowsill myself and touch the small, sharp toes, the hinge of knucklebone, the soft whisper of rabbit fur.

I miss Bill, and I miss the scrap of the past where we knew each other and belonged together. And I miss the future we never got to have. I miss the real possibility of a happy ending. I miss the invention of a machine that will turn wrong action back into thought, anger back to love.

It is fair to say that I never recovered from that summer at the Weyburn Mental Hospital. I am not the self

I was before Bill killed Henry Tudor. I am happier now. But the strange thing is that I remember the past as more true, not less, with each passing year. It's not that events are sharper, but that they're more full of feeling. It's as if the events themselves have sloughed off their chronology and exist now only as pure emotion.

It was thought that Henry Tudor had run off and was hiding in the hospital stables because he'd seen me come into the mattress factory to take Rusty Kirk away, and perhaps he assumed that all of the men would be taken away, one by one, that his turn would come and he didn't want to disappear from the only place where he felt safe. He was probably hiding from me because he feared me, and when he saw me in the stables, he might have thought that I had found him, that I was coming to capture him and to take him away from the Weyburn. When he was advancing towards me over the stable floor, he was most likely surrendering. He certainly wasn't attacking me. Henry Tudor was disturbed, but he wasn't a violent man.

Bill, on the other hand, was a violent man. I knew this myself, and it was in his file, the one that Luke Christiansen had read out to me. Bill had mostly kept his violent urges under control at the Weyburn, but his attachment to me had tipped the balance.

I can't forgive myself for what happened to Bill. It was my doing entirely. I can see now that I hung on to him too tightly, that I forced a relationship on him that he perhaps didn't want or couldn't handle. Henry Tudor's death, and Bill's too, can only be my fault.

But I had wanted to help Bill, to genuinely help him. He had given me hope and love when I had none, and I wanted to return that kindness. I wanted that very badly.

What do you owe the person who has saved you?

You owe them everything.

These are the last green fields of August. From the top of Sugar Hill they shine like emeralds in the sun, unnaturally brilliant in the way things are the moment before they start to fade.

WHEN I GET back to the house, it's coming on supper-time. My mother doesn't remark on how long I've been gone. We sit down at the kitchen table, eat cold meat pie and boiled potatoes, listening to the deep notes of the male news announcer as he talks calmly about the day's events and recounts the weather forecast.

I'm restless from the funeral and the talk with Lucy Weber, from the walk up to the top of Sugar Hill, and all the thoughts in my head, the feelings in my body. After supper, I leave my mother on the porch and go for a walk down the dusty driveway. I walk out to the cross-roads and back again, the fields growing golden with the setting sun, the neighbouring farms set back from the road, exactly where I remember them. Here in the prairies, it is the sky that changes. What's on the ground tends to stay put.

There's the click of insects in the grasses at the edge of the road, and every so often a truck will clatter past, leaving a tumbleweed of dust boiling in the air behind it.

When I get back to the house, my mother is still sitting on the porch, and so I go to sit down beside her.

"The evenings are going to get cooler soon," she says.

"Yes, I've been thinking that too."

"It's funny how the change happens, how it just comes on all of a sudden, even though you expect it to be gradual. But it never is. One day you just wake up and it's coming on winter."

"Yes. It always surprises me too."

We're quiet for a while.

"It's been a long, troubling day, hasn't it?" my mother says.

"It has."

"But it's a peaceful evening."

"Yes."

"Do you see that spot?" My mother points to the ground just in front of the truck. "That's where he fell. Just tipped off the porch and staggered for a bit, then dropped right there. He was on his way into town, to the hardware for some roofing shingles." She pauses. "He was face down in the dirt. I let him lie there for a good long time before I called the ambulance. Just to make sure. I watched from behind the curtains at the living room window. When the birds started landing on him, I knew for certain he was dead."

"Mom."

"I thought it would have happened sooner, with all the drink." She looks at me and her eyes are bright. "I should have done more, tried harder to get you free of him."

"Mom, it's okay." I reach over and take her hand. "Honestly it is." Her hand is as small as a child's in mine. "I don't blame you. Because, in a strange way, I was free of him."

We sit for a long time like that, holding hands on the porch, while the daylight thins and the night begins to come on and the moon drags her light across the fields.

I TAKE A taxi home from the airport. It's been raining, and the streets shine and hiss as we drive over them. All the brightness of the city seems alarming after the emptiness of the prairie.

Maggie opens the door for me. She must have been watching for my taxi through the front window.

"How was it?" she asks, leaning up to kiss me.

"Brutal. For the most part."

I put my suitcase down in the hall.

"But then better."

"How was your mother?"

"She was okay. It was good to see her."

"I'm glad." Maggie puts her arms around me. "I know you weren't looking forward to it."

"Well, it had to be done, and seeing her was nicer than I'd expected. Maybe we'll take Sarah out there for a visit at the holidays? After my mother has moved into town."

"I think that's a great idea."

I'm hungry and start down the hallway to the kitchen, but Maggie holds on to my arm.

"Before you do anything else, you should go and say good night to Sarah. She's been waiting up for you."

I take the stairs two at a time. Past the landing window, where the tops of the maples rise above the neighbour's roofline. Past the bathroom door with its stained-glass transom of a tiny bird perched delicately on a branch.

Sarah is awake.

"You're back, Daddy."

"I am."

"It felt long."

"Yes. For me too."

I cross the room and sit down on the edge of her bed.

"Shall we have a story now you're home?" she says in such a grown-up way that it makes me smile.

"Sure. Which one?"

"My favourite."

I don't need to open a book to tell this story. This story I know by heart. This story I will always know by heart.

"Bill never likes to leave town the same way twice," I say. "He strides out with an urgency I find hard to match. He leads me through the tamarack woods. He leads me through the meadow bog. He leads me through the tall prairie grasses."

The breeze blowing in the window is warm, fragrant with night flowers. If I close my eyes, I can imagine it is the house in Canwood and I am a boy again, stepping down off the front porch, on my way to Sugar Hill.

AUTHOR'S NOTE

THIS STORY IS based on a murder that took place in Canwood, Saskatchewan, in 1947, and on the LSD drug trials that were undertaken in the Weyburn Mental Hospital through the 1950s. Although I have taken details of the murder from the historical record, and used the line of questioning from the transcripts of the preliminary trial, this novel tries to be faithful not to these things but to the memory of one Hugh Lafave, who was a boy in Canwood at the time of the murder and was later a superintendent at the Weyburn Mental Hospital. Hugh knew the murderer, a man known locally as Rabbit Foot Bill.

ACKNOWLEDGEMENTS

I WOULD LIKE to thank my agent, Clare Alexander, and my editor, Jennifer Lambert, for their encouragement and assistance. The book is better because of their efforts and belief in the story. Thanks also to managing editorial director Noelle Zitzer.

The Provincial Archives of Saskatchewan hold the trial documents paraphrased in this novel. I would like to thank them for providing me with a copy of them.

Hugh Lafave has spent years recounting his story of Rabbit Foot Bill to me, and this book wouldn't exist without him or without the support and enthusiasm of Carol Drake. I am indebted to both of them and grateful for the time we've spent together.

Thanks to the people who make my life work: Mary Louise Adams, Nancy Jo Cullen, Eleanor MacDonald, Kirsteen MacLeod, Susan Olding, Marco Reiter, Sarah Tsiang. Thanks, Charlotte.

For this book, I would particularly like to thank Su Rynard, who collaborated with me on an earlier version of this story in the form of a screenplay. Most of what works in the novel is thanks to her and to our long and considered discussions about truth and fiction.

BIBLIO OTTAWA LIBRARY

3 2950 71669 078 7